To Sunnie,
Best of everything
always!
Anthony Bjorklund

EVICTED!

ANTHONY BJORKLUND

2

To my family and friends.
Thank you for not making fun of me when I told
you for the umpteenth time in my life
that I'd started another book.
And for any of you who did thank you
for doing so behind my back.

Prologue

The planet Earth hung beautifully in the black void of space, a blue and green oasis in the middle of a desert of nothingness. It orbited the Sun at just the right distance to provide warmth for its humans inhabitants, but not so close as to turn them all into crispy critters. It rotated on its axis fast enough to keep everyone firmly rooted on its surface, but not so fast that it squashed everyone into pancakes or made baseball impossible to play no matter how many steroids were taken. This spinning also kept a rich atmosphere comprised of seventy-one percent nitrogen, twenty-one percent oxygen, one percent argon, and point zero-zero-four percent carbon dioxide wrapped around the globe, a most nurturing mixture of gases.

There was plenty of thirst quenching water to be found on the planet's surface to keep the humans from drying out which also held a wealth of food in the form of fish and crustaceans. Green plants grew abundantly, keeping the delicate climate's balance in check while providing wood to build shelters and rocking chairs, and lettuce and cucumbers to make salads. Thousands of furry, feathered and scaly animals scurried about, many of whom the humans hunted and cooked over fires or skinned and wore to keep warm. Unfortunately some of these also got pushed into extinction, but that's what they got for being either too useful or in humanity's way.

The humans eventually discovered there were vast treasure troves buried under their feet. They excavated stone and metal to build giant cities to live in to get on each other's

5

nerves more efficiently and dug up coal to burn so they could watch CSI and condition their air. Walking began to seem like an awful chore so they manufactured millions upon millions of automobiles to ride around and talk on their cell phones in. Of course all those cars had to run on something so they sucked oil out of the ground which was great because it gave them something new to fight over and spill into the oceans.

The Earth didn't mind all the human's improvements at first. It didn't have much to say in the matter anyway being just a planet and all that. But it did have things set up a certain way and when they began adding chemicals to the air, soil and water that had no business being there while chopping down huge chunks of its oxygen providing forests it began to toss out more and more hurricanes and blizzards like a cow swishing its tail to remove a biting insect. The Earth wasn't trying to be mean. Again, it was just a planet. But this was the only way it knew to try and get things back in balance. And maybe, just maybe, let people know they were getting a little too rowdy up on the surface.

But humans being humans they ignored the Earth's warning signs and continued bettering life. And while there was a fair amount of debate about actually doing something about the environment no one could find any rock solid proof there was anything wrong with it other than vast stretches of polar ice caps melting and holes in ozone layers. They didn't see any reason to get on the bus with a bunch of other humans without said proof when they all had such nice Humvees and Ram trucks with hemis sitting out in their driveways. So in spite of the efforts of a few pesky Al

6

Goreans the planet had to limp along and do the best it could to continue to provide the finest in human care despite a few hundred billion tons of pollutants in its environment.

Then one day the Earth finally got a little outside help that would change things forever, and one human who was not any differently different from the rest of the humans found himself unexpectedly and reluctantly smack in the middle of it all.

His name is Jake Williams and his part in the story begins more or less here.

Chapter One

Jake lay in his bed peacefully sleeping. He felt an odd sensation, almost like a primal fear, and woke with a start. He opened his eyes and found a pair of feline ones looking down at him.

"Damn it, Ray," said Jake. "I thought we talked about this. I promised not to get you fixed and you promised to stop scaring the hell out of me every morning."

Jake's cat licked it's lips and continued to stare at him.

"Not to mention it makes me wonder how long you've been there and what you've been doing all that time," said Jake. "Probably performing some crazy cat ritual or something. Now scram and go do something useful like finding that family of mice that keeps getting into my frosted flakes."

Ray jumped off the bed and padded out of the room, his mission accomplished.

Jake rolled over and checked out his alarm clock which read just past eleven. He got out of bed and stretched, feeling good after being able to sleep in on a Thursday even if it meant he had a three hour drive ahead of him. He went into the bathroom and did all the things necessary to interact with other humans without having them recoil in disgust, then packed a few toiletries and carried them and the rest of his previously suitcased belongings into the living room.

He went into the kitchen and whipped up a quick breakfast of fruit, oatmeal and toast then sat down and ate while reading the paper and discussing the news with Ray.

"It says here that we're in for some warm weather again this weekend," said Jake. "Good time for me to get out of Chicago. Of course you'll be staying here and chilling in the central air. You wouldn't like it where I'm going anyway. I don't know if they have fluoridation so the toilet water would probably taste funny to you. Besides, I don't want you running around with those country cats then come back here and start line dancing or something."

The fat grey tabby meowed a complaint.

"It's not like I'm leaving you here all on your own you know," said Jake. "Ms. Angela from across the hall is going to come over and take care of you. If you play your cards right and look a little lonely she might take you over to her place and you can spend some quality time with her Siamese that I know you've had your eyes on. Just be safe. You don't want to get tied down with a wife and kittens. Trust me, it always ends the same. She'll get the cat box and all your cat toys in the settlement and you'll be sitting here all alone getting looped on catnip to ease the pain."

Jake Williams knew about such things, being one of Chicago's most successful young divorce lawyers. At twenty-nine he already had a thriving practice which had netted him a nice apartment, a custom Humvee, and more than a few dates with lawyer wife wannabees. A tall, good looking black man who dressed with style and carried himself with confidence and charm, Jake considered himself a pretty successful and happy single guy.

Jake got up and put his dishes in the dishwasher and pulled a grey sports jacket over the black tee and tan slacks he was wearing. He picked up his bags and went over to the door, opened it, and stopped to say goodbye to Ray.

"So look, I'll be back in a few days unless something goes wrong and they need me for a quick divorce right after the wedding," said Jake. "And you better still be single when I get back." Ray gave him a *go already so I can start getting into things* look and Jake exited the apartment, closed and locked the door and took the elevator down to the parking garage. He walked across the pavement to his beloved black Humvee and pushed the button on his car remote and the alarm chirped back at him and unlocked the doors. Moments later the engine roared to life and soon Jake and the vehicle were exiting the garage into heavy traffic on Twenty-Third Avenue.

They battled their way from the heart of downtown past the Picasso and Wrigley Field and inched their way out of the Chicago metropolitan area and into the Milwaukee metropolitan area. They headed west and eventually found the open highway and began to make some time while Jake conducted business on his cell phone. They passed through Madison and continued on, farm after farm passing by, until an hour or so later a friendly sign appeared that read *Welcome to Annandale.*

The Humvee rumbled down the tiny main street and Jake spotted what he was looking for and pulled into an open parking spot. He got out of the car and took off his sunglasses and looked around him and smiled, a little amused at the quaint scene around him. "Wow, welcome to Mayberry. This is usually all in black and white," he said. "I wonder what Deputy Fife is up to."

It was a beautiful, warm summers day in the little town of Annandale Wisconsin. People passed by, many of whom looked like farmers, making their way in and out of the small stores along the tree lined street. Most of them stared at Jake who seemed a little out of place standing next to his urban assault vehicle dressed in his hip sports jacket and slacks.

The door to Anderson Family Law opened and Steve Anderson came out wearing a maroon polo shirt and a pair of jeans. He waved at Jake and came towards him and Jake smiled and waved in reply.

"Jake! You made it. Guess my directions got you here," said Steve.

"Yeah they were a big help," said Jake. "Drive to Annandale, stop the car."

"Hey it worked didn't it? Great to see you," said Steve. He and Jake shook hands and gave each other a manly hug.

"So this is your new office huh?" said Jake, motioning towards the nearby building. "Any big cases yet? Gonna help Oly get custody of his blue ribbon hog from Lena?"

"Ha ha," said Steve. "I suppose you're going to start in with the small town jokes right away?"

"Yeah, can't think of any reason to wait," said Jake.

"Great. Looking forward to it," said Steve. "So how was the drive?"

"Long and full of cows," said Jake.

"That's Wisconsin for you," said Steve.

"Made me hungry," said Jake.

"You wanna go grab a bite to eat?" asked Steve.

"Yeah man. They got a McDonalds here?" said Jake.

"Nope," said Steve.

"Burger King?" asked Jake.

"Nada," said Steve.

Jake put his sunglasses back on and looked down over them at Steve. "All that beef roaming around and I can't get a burger?" he said. "I mean you do eat here don't you? Aside from all the barbecuing."

"Yeah, usually we eat at the diner," said Steve. He started to walk down the sidewalk. "Follow me. It's just down the street."

Jake looked around him, then followed. "Of course it's just down the street," he said. "If it wasn't just down the street it'd be out of town, wouldn't it? Steve?"

Jake and Steve sat in a booth by the window in the small old fashioned diner. A hand-made sign advertised the Wednesday night spaghetti feed. A few customers ate at tables around the room and on bar stools at the counter. Steve read a copy of the local newspaper while Jake finished his club sandwich.

Steve was an average looking likeable guy in his late twenties. While there was nothing that stood out about him everyone felt at ease around him. Standing about five foot ten with brown hair he could blend into a crowd yet everyone remembered the nice guy they had met at the party. He and Jake had been friends since they attended law school together in Chicago.

"Man we are so doomed," said Steve while looking at the paper.

"Not the doomed thing again," said Jake.

"Well we are," said Steve.

"Yeah so you keep saying. What now?" said Jake.

"Take a look at this," said Steve while handing the newspaper to Jake.

Jake took it and read out loud. *"One day only. All sofas and recliners thirty percent off.* You're right, Stevie, I think I see the Four Horsemen coming down main street," he said, looking out the window.

"Not that, you idiot," said Steve. "Further down."

Jake read from the newspaper again.

"Corn prices in May down three percent from April," said Jake. "Good thing I had my money in pork bellies."

"Give me that," said Steve, exasperated. He reached over and snatched the paper out of Jake's hands and swatted him on the head with it, then read from it.

"This. *Scientists said that last week a twenty-three mile long strip of the arctic shelf broke off near Greenland,"* said Steve.

"So?" said Jake.

"So? That's huge! That's almost from here to Appleton. Imagine if that fell into the ocean," said Steve.

"Man that'd be a whole lot of cows," said Jake. "Hey can cows swim?"

"Yeah they can but--" began Steve.

"Phew. Good. That's a load off my mind," said Jake.

"Look, forget about the cows," said Steve, shaking the newspaper at Jake. "Doesn't this worry you? I mean, this is going on all the time. The temperature just keeps on rising."

"Good," said Jake. "Maybe someday we won't have to freeze our asses off when we make it to a Bears game."

"Packers game," said Steve.

"Whatever," said Jake. "Look, the point is all this global warming stuff is probably just Mother Nature going through one of her cycle things."

"And if it isn't?" said Steve.

"Then there'll be a whole lot of bronze women with uber tans running around," said Jake.

"Man, you're hopeless," said Steve.

"Yeah, you keep saying that too," said Jake.

Steve put the newspaper down. "Anyway. So how have you been, Jake? Still bleeding the soon to be divorced dry?"

"That's what us divorce lawyer vampire types do," said Jake. "You still getting married?"

"This Saturday. Nice of you to show up by the way," said Steve.

Jake reached into his jacket pocket and took out a business card holder, then opened it and took out one of his cards and slid it across the table towards Steve. "Here's my card. I'll give you a friends discount."

Steve gave Jake and the card a dirty look and Jake laughed.

"No seriously man. I'm sure you two will do fine," said Jake. "Besides, you have my number already."

"Yeah, unless Cynthia erases it. She thinks you're a bad influence," said Steve.

"And I didn't think she liked me," said Jake. He stood up and picked up the check off the table, got out his wallet and put the bill and some money on the table. "I got this."

Steve got out of the booth and stood up. "Thanks, Jake," he said.

"No problem. You're getting married. You're going to need all the money you can get," said Jake. He went out the door to the street and Steve followed him.

"So that's it huh?" said Jake, stopping out on the sidewalk. "You're going to get married and practice law here in Smallville and chase tractors instead of ambulances?"

"Something like that, yeah," said Steve.

"Wow. Guess I just don't get it. One minute you're living in Chicago working for a small and almost prestigious law firm, well on your way to a trophy wife, and suddenly you meet a horticulture student and you're head over heels in love with a 4H Club member," said Jake.

"That's how it happens sometimes I guess. Cynthia's a great gal," said Steve.

"I'm not saying she isn't. But couldn't she be an even greater gal and move to Chicago where all the action is?" said Jake.

"The family farm is here," said Steve. "Since Cynthia's parents passed away well...there was no way she was moving to Chicago. Besides, I like it here too, Jake. It's peaceful. You should try it for a while."

"Sorry I don't look good in plaid or hunter's orange," said Jake. "As soon as I get you all shackled up I'm going to see how fast I can get back to Chicago where the cars are honking, the money's flowing and the women all have long legs."

"Hi, Steve," said a rather attractive female voice that made Jake's libido want to know who it belonged to. He turned and found its owner was a tall overly attractive red-head wearing a blue halter top and cut-off jeans pasted over the top of a pair of lengthy tanned legs.

"Hey, Paula," said Steve as she walked past.

Paula gave Steve a little wave and looked Jake over then continued down the sidewalk a ways before turning into the local shoe store.

Jake watched her stroll away with interest, marveling again at the simple wonders of denim.

"You were saying?" said Steve.

"Yeah but if I lived here she'd just turn out to be my cousin," said Jake.

"Like that would stop you," said Steve.

"So. What are we doing tonight again?" said Jake.

"You're the one that supposed to know. You are the best man," said Steve.

"Yeah, well my plan got nixed," said Jake.

"Cynthia didn't think it was a good idea," said Steve.

"Uh-huh. What are we doing instead?" said Jake.

"Well we're going bowling for starters," said Steve.

"Yeah that beats the hell out of being carted around Chicago in a limo to watch gorgeous women toss their clothes around the room," said Jake. "And I could have sworn I've made my feelings about bowling abundantly clear."

"You have, but it's time to face your fears," said Steve. He slapped Jake on the shoulder. "Come on. Let's go get you settled in at the ranch. Then it's party time."

Chapter Two

It was a busy night at Bill's Bar, Bowling and Karaoke. Bill stood behind the bar making drinks while a cute blonde waitress named Shelly moved through the room delivering them. Steve was up at the bar getting beers and talking to Paula, the woman he and Jake had seen earlier on the street.

Jake stood in lane three, ball in hand, concentrating. He looked determined and gracefully rolled the ball towards the pins but it curved off almost instantly to the left and into the gutter. He gave the alley a dirty look then turned and walked back towards Tommy and Craig.

"A little more to the right, Jake," said Tommy, a red-haired freckled faced young man who was stuck with the thankless task of being Steve's usher.

"Hey, how am I supposed to bowl with him singing?" said Jake gesturing towards Mark, a slightly chunky man in a cowboy hat who was another member of the wedding party. Mark was up at the karaoke machine, microphone in hand, belting out a drunken off-key version of *I've Got Friends In Low Places*.

"Concentrate," said Craig, another of Steve's local friends who was blonde and fit the mold of the average mid-western Norwegian.

"I am concentrating. At least as much as I can while wearing someone else's shoes," said Jake.

Jake waited for his ball to pop out of the ball return then picked it up and started to step up to bowl again but saw a small boy was ready in lane four and motioned for him to go first. The boy rolled the ball slowly down the lane granny style and got a strike and went into a lengthy celebration dance. Jake looked at him sideways then stepped up and bowled and managed to knock down the ten pin. He turned, walked back and sat down and gave his red and green shoes an accusatory look. "It's all your fault," he said to them.

Steve walked down from the bar with a handful of beers and handed one to Jake. "Game over?" he said. "What did you end up getting?"

"You mean besides athletes foot?" said Jake. He pointed up to where the scores were projected. "It's up there where everyone can see it. No secrets in bowling."

Steve checked out Jake's score. "You're getting better. At least you scored higher than your age that time," he said.

"I saw you ran into that red-head again," said Jake.

"Who, Paula?" said Steve. "She asked about you. She said you were hot."

Jake looked up by the bar and found Paula was still there, checking him out. "She probably hasn't seen anything this refined her whole life, the poor thing."

Paula waved at Jake and he flashed a smile and gave her a cute little wave back. Then she picked a bag up off the bar and headed towards the exit.

"Damn, she's getting away!" said Jake.

"Don't worry, you'll see her again. She's in the wedding," said Steve. "She just stopped in to pick up some wine coolers for Cynthia's bachelorette party."

"She's in the wedding?" asked Jake. "You could tell me these things sooner. It should be like *hey Jake we're going bowling but there's going to be this sexy woman in the wedding party.* You know, keep the scales balanced."

"I'll see what I can do in the future," said Steve.

Mark finished singing and came down to join the others. "What did you think of my song, Jake?" he asked.

"I think the Japanese sure got even with us for the bomb with the whole karaoke thing," said Jake, taking a sip of his beer.

"That's what I like about you, Jake," said Mark. "You're a funny guy. Isn't he a funny guy, Tommy?"

"Very funny guy," agreed Tommy.

"Yeah. Very funny guy," said Mark. "Shelly!" he shouted. "Another round of shots over here!"

Johnny the local skateboarder walked by at that moment, finished with the video game he'd been playing over in the corner. "Dude! Did I hear something about shots?"

"And one for Johnny," yelled Mark.

"Thanks dude," said Johnny.

"How's it hanging, Johnny?" asked Steve.

"Couldn't be better dude!" said Johnny. "Pulled a backside Nollie 360 on my board today. It was so gnarly!"

"Sounds bitchin'," said Jake.

"Totally dude," said Johnny.

"Johnny, this is Jake Williams. He's here from Chicago to be my best man," said Steve. "Jake, Johnny."

Johnny and Jake exchanged a complicated handshake. "Good to meet you bro," said Johnny.

"Dude," said Jake.

Johnny was twenty-three years old and still lived with his mother. He had long, blondish hair that stuck out from under the red bandanna he always wore on his head. His Tony Hawke t-shirt was missing it's sleeves and his ratty blue jeans were missing their knees. He was on the short side and stayed slender due to his busy schedule despite a healthy diet of Snickers bars, nacho cheese Doritos and Red Bull. He skateboarded in the afternoon, partied in the evening, played video games all night then slept through the morning before starting the whole cycle over again. With so many full days it was no wonder he rarely found time for mundane tasks like work.

Shelly arrived with the shots and put them down on the table. "You can bring the tab too, Shelly," said Steve.

"You guys leaving, Steve?" said Shelly.

"Yeah, we leaving, Steve?" said Jake somewhat sarcastically.

"Sorry to break your heart," said Steve. He turned to Shelly. "Ignore Jake. He's fun impaired."

Shelly eyed Jake up and down with interest. "Too bad," she said, then left to get their bill.

The guys gathered around and they each picked up a shot glass and Craig raised his to make a toast. "To Steve and Cynthia," he said. "May the road go uphill to meet you. No wait. May the wind behind you always...no that's not it either. Okay. How about this. May you never find Cynthia in the back seat of a Chevy with--"

Jake interrupted him. "Nip it!" he said. "We'll just nip that in the bud. Sit down before you hurt someone. Got to do everything around here myself." He thought for a moment before speaking. "May your life together with

Cynthia be filled with all the happiness, warmth and love the world can give to you."

Jake paused as if finished and everyone started to drink but stopped as he continued again.

"And when that runs out be sure and give me a call before Cynthia does or I'll make sure she gets your truck," said Jake.

Everyone clinked their glasses together and cheered then drank down their shots.

Steve came over to Jake, feigning teary eyed and sniffling. "That was beautiful, man. I love you," he said, then tried to give Jake a big hug.

Jake put up his hands to defend himself. "Hey hey now. None of that," he said. "No manly hugs tonight please. And you think you're crying now, just wait till you're married."

Shelly came over with the tab and Jake got out his wallet and paid her while everyone grabbed their belongings and prepared to leave.

"You know you don't have to pay for everything, Jake," said Steve.

Jake pointed to himself. "Divorce lawyer," he said, then pointed at Steve. "Pig lawyer."

"Hey can I come with you guys?" asked Johnny hopefully.

"No!" said everyone in unison except Jake.

"Duuudes!" said Johnny, crestfallen.

"Sorry man, I was pulling for you," said Jake.

Johnny wandered off to look for someone else to buy him a drink.

"Where are we going now?" Jake asked Steve.

"Bonfire time," said Steve.

"Out to the farm huh?" said Jake. "Did you pick up the marshmallows and the graham crackers? And the Hershey bars?"

"No but we do have a keg," said Steve.

"Damn. Don't you know anything about bachelor parties? How are we supposed to make smores?" asked Jake.

"Come on smart guy," said Steve as he went out the door.

"You can't have a decent bachelor party without smores!" complained Jake.

Chapter Three

It was a beautiful, clear Wisconsin night. A soft breeze blew through the trees as the crickets chirped happily away.

Cynthia's two story Norman Rockwell country farm house sat near the road on the front edge of the property, a dirt driveway leading up to it. A porch wrapped around the house, complete with hanging porch swing. A white wooden fence ran along the edge of the yard keeping the peacefully dozing black and white dairy cows out of the yard and in the pasture where they belonged.

A fire burned in a pit surrounded by lawn chairs beside the house. Jake and Steve sat next to one another, watching the fire and drinking beers.

Jake looked up at the sky. "Nice night. A lot of stars."

Steve, who was moderately intoxicated, tipped his chair on its back two legs while rocking it. "Yeah there sure are," he agreed.

"I gotta say this is nice. So quiet," said Jake.

"Glad you like it," said Steve.

"Speaking of quiet, where did the rest of the boys go?" asked Jake.

"They went to say *hi* to the cows," said Steve.

"You're kidding right? Cynthia finds out she's gonna be p.o.'d," said Jake.

"Oh they're not messing with Cynthia's cows, they're too afraid of her. They're over at Craig's place just down the road," explained Steve. "I doubt if we'll see them again tonight."

"Well I hope they all get sat on," said Jake. "I mean, I wonder how they'd like it? Poor cow is just standing there snoozing away, dreaming about getting jiggy with some hot bull and all of a sudden wham, she's lying on the ground wondering what the hell happened and how she's going to get back up again."

"I thought you didn't like cows," said Steve, yawning.

"I don't, but that doesn't mean I think someone should be knocking them over just because they're too stupid to lie down and sleep like everyone else," said Jake.

There was a quiet moment. Jake stirred the fire with a stick while Steve leaned way back in his chair and looked up at the night sky.

"Wow. I think I see a UFO," said Steve.

Jake looked up. "Where?" he said.

Steve tipped his chair too far back and fell with a crash, legs flailing in the air as Jake calmly watched.

"Never mind, it's just a satellite," said Steve from the ground.

"You need some help?" said Jake.

"No I think I'll just stay down here a while," said Steve. "Kind of comfortable."

"Suit yourself," said Jake.

The two sat quietly, Steve looking up at the stars through glazed eyes from his back, Jake trying to decide if now was a good time to talk to Steve. He decided it was. "Hey, Steve," he said.

Steve yawned. "Hey, Jake," he said.

"I've got something I've been wanting to say to you," said Jake.

"Go for it," said Steve.

"You know how I always give you a hard time about getting hitched to Cynthia and all that?" said Jake.

"You mean like the time you tied me to a chair and threatened to shave off my mullet if I didn't come to my senses and break off the engagement?" asked Steve sleepily.

"No, that was actually pretty stupid," said Jake. "If you would have come to your senses I wouldn't have shaved off your mullet. Then I would have had to turn around and tie you back to the chair again until you came to your senses and let me shave off your mullet."

"Then what are you talking about?" said Steve, barely audible.

"All those other times," said Jake. "Saying you were making a big mistake marrying Cynthia. Telling you you were out of your mind and you should stay in Chicago. Although I still think you two should do that."

Jake paused to wait for Steve to say something but he didn't.

"Well I just wanted to say I was wrong. About everything but Chicago. And to tell you I'm happy for you," continued Jake. "You know, finding someone to spend your life with. Raising a family, all that jazz. You're my best friend and I want the best for you. I love you man."

There was no answer from Steve.

"You got the right idea. I mean all I got is an endless stream of gorgeous women going in and out of my apartment. What kind of life is that for a guy?" said Jake.

"It's been making me wonder. Maybe I should settle down too. Find the right girl like you did. Do you think I'm ready?"

Steve remained silent and Jake looked down at Steve to see what was going on. "Yo, Steve," he said.

Steve began to snore where he lay on the ground.

"I'll take that as a no. Thanks for the support," said Jake. He stood up. "Gonna go use the men's room. Let me know if you need anything."

Jake walked away from the bonfire and house towards a small group of bushes next to the white pasture fence. He stopped, looked around him, then unzipped his fly and prepared to do his business. He was looking down when he heard an odd humming sound, quiet at first but gradually growing louder. It appeared to be coming from above him and he looked up to see what it was. He squinted, not sure what he was seeing, then his eyes grew wide as he stared at the glowing light coming down from the sky.

He knew what it was right away of course. He'd seen plenty of movies and knew if you were standing in the middle of nowhere or at least close to it and a light began to come down from the sky as this one was now, you pretty much had to figure it was a spaceship. That didn't mean that he believed it either but there it was, a shiny, silver, perfectly round orb about fifty feet in diameter lit with pulsating blue lights going on and off in sequence around the center of the ship.

Jake stared upwards at it in amazement, his face lit with a pale blue glow as the ship passed overhead. He watched as it floated quietly towards the pasture and

26

descended closer to the surface of the planet. It began to slow down and three beams of blue light emanated from its underside forming a tripod of sorts. The craft finally came to a gentle landing thirty or so yards away from Jake floating about five feet off the ground, apparently held there by the beams of light.

Mesmerized Jake walked over to the gate in the fence and opened it and walked towards the ship, his mouth hanging open in awe. He stopped a short distance away and cocked his head to one side and stared, puzzled and unsure of what to do next. As he looked on a silver metallic ramp about six feet wide elegantly slid outwards from the craft. It had curved sides like a water slide and extended itself all the way to the ground. An arched door materialized above the ramp which slid open from bottom to top and Jake shaded his eyes as bright light spilled from the interior. The outline of a small humanoid appeared in the doorway standing about five feet tall. It moved down the ramp, walking very upright and somewhat stiffly, carrying a small cylinder of some kind in one hand.

The being wore no clothing but since it was built like a doll it really had no need for it, despite what clothes horse Barbie might have thought. It had bright yellow skin topped with no hair of any kind, mop top or eyebrow. Two cylindrically shaped solid black eyes bracketed a small nose above a small mouth. Tiny ears stuck out from its head.

The alien reached the bottom of the ramp and stopped to look around. It didn't notice Jake and instead walked towards a nearby cow and looked it up and down, seemingly puzzled.

"Are you sentient?" the being asked the cow in a bored sounding monotone.

The cow looked blankly back at him and chose not to answer, annoyed at having been awakened by the ship's lights.

"I said, are you sentient?" repeated the being, determined to illicit a response. It got none and became irritated and looked around, it's eyes coming to rest on Jake before moving towards him.

As the being drew closer Jake suddenly began to wonder if remaining in the area had been that bright an idea. The little creature looked harmless enough but then again so did all the aliens in movies right up until the point where they suddenly became nasty and drew a laser pistol and fired, turning you to ashes to begin their campaign to wipe out your species and plunder your planet's resources. He thought about turning and running off to the farmhouse or at least trying to rouse Steve for whatever help he might be but found himself riveted to the spot. The being came to within a few feet of him and stopped, looking him up and down while Jake did the same back.

"Are you sentient?" the being asked Jake.

It didn't occur to Jake to be offended by being quizzed in the same manner as a cow and he simply said "What?" a bit dazed and confused by the whole thing, not to mention a little buzzed from celebratory shots and beer.

"Are you sentient?" asked the being, annoyed at having to ask the same question for the fourth time. "Knowing that you exist and wondering why?"

"Yeah I think so," said Jake, uncertain at this point.

"I wish he'd prep me better for these things," said the being irritably. "It would have helped to at least know what you humans look like." It took hold of a thin metal rod running down the side of the cylinder it was carrying and pulled it out and away and a lit screen pulled out behind it like an electronic scroll.

"Name?" asked the being.

"My name?" asked Jake.

"No my name. I came all the way to your planet so we could stand and play guessing games all night," said the being sarcastically. "Of course your name!"

"Okay, okay," said Jake, a bit chagrined. "Jake."

"Jake. Is that your first, middle and last name? Is it Jake Jake Jake or just Jake?" said the being.

"No, it's Jake Williams," said Jake.

The being spoke while typing on the electronic scroll. "Social security number?" it asked.

"Social security number?" asked Jake.

"Is there an echo in here?" said the being.

"You mean out here," said Jake, determined to get some control over the conversation.

"No I mean in this environment. Don't correct me. Unlike you creatures I always say what I mean," said the being. "Now give me your social security number."

"Fine. Seven-four-five, nine-two, four-eight-six-three," said Jake.

The being entered the numbers onto the pad then moved towards Jake and held the scroll out towards him while pointing at it. "Now place your right thumb onto the oval," it said.

Jake paused, looking at the brightly colored screen, then did as he was told. The being tapped on the scroll twice and pulled on the electronic page and it came away from the rest of the cylinder and rolled itself into a neat tube similar to the original and the being handed it to Jake who reluctantly took it.

"What's this?" asked Jake.

"Your copy. You have been served. Have a nice day," said the being. It turned and started walking back towards the ship.

"What?" asked Jake sharply and the being stopped and turned back to face him.

"Have a nice day. Or night. Or not. Whichever you prefer," said the alien. It turned again and continued towards the ramp.

Jake shook himself and came out of the fog his head had been mired in. "Wait a minute! Hold it right there," he demanded. "What do you mean I've been served?"

The being ignored him and moved across the pasture.

"You! Alien dude. I'm talking to you!" said Jake, louder this time. "What do you mean I've been served? Is that some sort of threat? You going to eat me now? Dip me in some hot sauce?"

The little alien kept his back turned and went up the ramp.

"Come back here!" shouted Jake.

As the being reached the doorway of the ship it stopped and turned to face Jake. "By the way your fly is open," it said, matter-of-factly.

Jake stared at the alien then looked down. "Damn it," he said before fixing the problem. The being walked into the ship and the door slid down shut behind him.

Jake stood breathing heavily from excitement and shouting and stared at the ship. "Yeah you better hide," he said.

Steve walked up behind him, yawning. "What's all the shouting about?" he asked calmly.

"Well what would you be doing if an alien just served you?" asked Jake.

"Depends on what was on the menu," said Steve.

Jake pointed at the ship. "Are you blind?"

"Oh that," said Steve, dismissing it. "That's just a dream. Go away and let me look for Jessica Alba."

Jake reached out slapped Steve hard across the face.

"Ow," said Steve, not so calmly.

"Yeah ow," said Jake.

"Hey that shouldn't hurt," said Steve.

"No it shouldn't," said Jake. "And you shouldn't be dreaming about Jessica Alba anymore either."

"You mean this isn't a dream?" said Steve.

"Not unless it's mine," said Jake.

"So Jessica isn't going to wander by for no apparently good reason?" said Steve.

"No she isn't," said Jake. "But Cynthia might."

"Well shouldn't we tell somebody?" said Steve.

"Who we going to tell? Your marriage counselor?" said Jake.

"Not about my dream!" said Steve.

"Oh you mean tell someone about that alien space ship sitting over there next to the cows," said Jake.

"Yeah that," said Steve.

"You got anyone in mind?" said Jake.

Steve thought for a moment. "I know. I'll call the sheriff," said Steve, turning and heading quickly towards the house.

"Good," said Jake, following. "Just be sure and tell him to give SETI a call because they might want to point a telescope or two at Cynthia's pasture."

Chapter Four

Jake and Steve sat at the big wooden table in the dining room. Or more precisely Steve sat at the table while Jake slumped over it, head lying on his arms trying desperately to stay awake, having given up on staring blankly at the daisies in the milk can centerpiece.

"Yes. That's right, a spaceship," said Steve into the telephone he was holding. He listened while the person on the other end answered him.

"Yeah. First contact made," Steve confirmed.

"Look, I'm telling you the truth." said Steve after a short pause. He waited and listened again.

"So you believe me. Good," said Steve.

"You're just not going to do anything about it," said Steve.

"Yeah. Yeah. I understand. Yep. Yep. Thanks a lot. You too. Good bye," said Steve, and he hung up the phone.

"So?" said Jake sleepily, head still firmly planted in the I could easily fall asleep position.

"So they don't care either," said Steve. "We've called the sheriff, the FBI, the CIA, NASA, the National Guard and the Enquirer. They're all interested and say they believe we have a spaceship outside but not enough to come here and do anything about it. Can you think of anyone else we could try?"

"Well, we could call the Coast Guard but we might be a little bit out of their jurisdiction," said Jake.

"What do you thinks' going on? Why won't anyone come here?" said Steve.

Jake put his head up and rubbed his eyes. "Well it is Wisconsin," he said. "Look, all I know is it's weird, it's late, I'm tired and I'm hung-over. I'm going to bed and hope this was all some sort of psychotic episode brought on by bowling." He stood up.

"How can you sleep at a time like this?" asked Steve.

"What am I supposed to do at a time like this? Go out and milk the cows?" said Jake. "No thanks, I don't want to shatter my illusion that milk comes from plastic jugs. Instead I'm going to lie down, close my eyes and snore. I'll see you in a few hours." He walked out of the room and headed towards the stairs.

"Ten bucks says you won't be able to sleep!" said Steve after him.

"I'm telling Cynthia you've got a gambling problem," said Jake from the other room. "And don't touch that scroll!"

Steve reached out and touched the scroll several times, then picked it up and examined it. "He won't be able to sleep," he said to himself.

Chapter Five

Jake lay sleeping in the comfy guest room, snoring loudly, mouth hanging open goofily as he drooled all over his pillow. A big homemade quilt was pulled up to his chin. Sunlight shown through the sheer curtains hanging over the window and inched it's way slowly across the floor. Several paintings of ducks stared at him from the walls, as did the naturally attractive brunette sitting in the overstuffed chair next to his bed. She was tall with long wavy hair and wore a white button down shirt and a pair of faded blue jeans.

Jake stirred and turned over onto his back, propped up by the big soft pillows on the bed. He yawned and smacked his lips and opened his eyes and blinked a couple of times. He rubbed those same eyes then froze as he noticed the woman sitting unexpectedly in his room.

"Hi," said Jake, which wasn't the best opening line of his career but was all he could muster at the moment.

"Hello," said the woman. "How did you sleep?"

"I don't know," said Jake. "I was too busy sleeping to notice." He looked the woman up and down and while he didn't mind doing it at all he was still perplexed. "Look, I don't want you to get the idea I don't like waking up with pretty women in my room or anything but who are you again?"

"Nicole Parks, maid of honor," she said.

Jake verified he was wearing his sweat pants under the covers then got out of bed and stood up. "Jake Williams, best man," he said. "Now we know who we are. Just have to figure out what you're doing in my room."

Nicole pulled a digital camera out of her front shirt pocket and held it up. "I wanted to talk to you about the alien. You see I'm a photo-journalist. At least I want to be. Right now I work for the Milwaukee Post. Classifieds. But that ship out there might be my chance for a big break," she explained.

"You mean it's still there?" said Jake. He went over to the window and pushed the curtain aside and looked out. To his dismay the ship was indeed still sitting there, unchanged, except now it was gleaming in the sunlight instead of the moonlight. "Damn. Bad enough it wasn't a dream, the least it could have done was fly away by now."

"Well it didn't, and since you were the one who made first contact last night I was hoping you'd let me follow you around and take some pictures," said Nicole. "You know, document what happens next."

Jake thought about it for a moment. "Okay. I'm about to go jump in the shower right now so if you want to follow me..."

"Uh, maybe we should start after that," said Nicole.

"Suit yourself. Thought you might want to snap some candid's and get a leg up on USA Today," said Jake.

Nicole stood up and went over to the doorway to leave the room. "Thanks for the offer but no. I'll be waiting downstairs. If you're hungry Cynthia's making a late lunch," she said.

"Late lunch?" said Jake, looking for his watch. "What time is it anyway?"

"About three," said Nicole.

"Wow. Guess I was tired," said Jake, picking his suitcase off the floor and putting it on the bed. "First contact must take something out of you."

Nicole started to go out of the room, then stopped halfway and leaned attractively against the door frame. "Yeah, Steve's been going crazy waiting for you to wake up. He wants to talk to you about that scroll," she said then went out into the hallway.

"I told him not to touch that," said Jake, unzipping his bag.

Nicole put her head back inside the door. "Well he did," she said, then left again.

Jake shook his head as he dug for something to wear. "Dude never listens to me. Even when I told him she was a he did he listen, noooo."

Nicole popped her head in the door again and looked at Jake quizzically.

"Mardi Gras. Believe me, you don't want to know," said Jake.

Nicole pulled her head back out of the door and went downstairs, even though she did.

Steve sat at the table in the dining room looking refreshed, having himself slept for a few hours. He had the scroll pulled open and was reading it, a finished plate of food sitting in front of him. Nicole sat across from him drinking a cup of coffee.

Cynthia was is in the kitchen making a sandwich for Jake who was just walking into the room and he went over to her and threw his arms open wide. "Cynthia! I didn't get to see you yesterday. How about a hug girl?"

"It's afternoon and why is there a spaceship sitting outside my house the day before I'm supposed to get married?" said Cynthia curtly, ignoring Jake's request for a squeeze.

"Hello to you too," said Jake. He gave up on schmoozing Cynthia for the moment and turned to Steve instead and found him puttering around with the scroll. "Thought I told you not to mess with that thing."

"You know I've been reading through this," said Steve. "It's a lot of legal mumbo jumbo..."

"Then shouldn't I be the one reading it?" asked Jake. "Never mind, I haven't had my coffee yet. Speaking of which..." he said then poured himself a cup. He walked into the dining room and sat down across from Steve next to Nicole.

"You forget I'm the one who got you through law school and all that legal mumbo jumbo," said Steve.

"Oh yeah. I just taught you how to pick up girls," said Jake. He looked and found Cynthia beside him holding a plate of food. She gave him a dirty look then plopped it down in front of him and went back into the kitchen. "Hey it worked on you, didn't it?" he said after her. He picked up his ham and Wisconsin Cheddar cheese sandwich and took a bite. "So what is the thing anyway?"

Steve glanced into the kitchen to make sure Cynthia was out of earshot then leaned across the table. "Well, it's a little confusing and I don't get everything it's talking about, but I'm pretty sure it's an eviction notice," he said quietly. "From Earth."

"An eviction notice?" hissed Jake. "What, I'm being kicked off the planet?"

"No, *we* are," said Steve.

"What do you mean?" said Nicole.

"I mean you, me, Jake, George Bush, Johnny Depp...everyone," said Steve.

"Well, Georgie might have it coming," said Jake. "But get real Steve, you must have read it wrong," he said, grabbing a potato chip off his plate.

"I'm telling you that's what it says," said Steve, motioning at the scroll.

"Give me that and let me take a look," said Jake, putting out his hand then quickly taking it back again. "Never mind, the coffee still hasn't kicked in."

Cynthia walked through the room heading towards the front door. "I'm going outside to make sure they're not vaporizing my livestock," she said and disappeared.

Nicole heard the front door open and close then said "Don't you think we should let Cynthia in on this too?"

"Of course," said Steve. "Just not quite yet. She's a wee bit wound up with the wedding right now and telling her our honeymoon might be on Pluto isn't liable to help much."

"Did the scroll say anything about *why* we're being evicted?" asked Jake.

"It's kind of sketchy on that point. Something about some environmental report," said Steve.

"So what do you think we should do anyway?" said Jake. "Since it doesn't look like we're going to get any outside help from any shady governmental organizations."

"I think you should go out and try to talk to them," said Steve.

"Me? Why me? I should only be going if you want me to try to get custody of the kids," protested Jake.

"Because it also says that the person served with this notice becomes the Representative of the Earth," said Steve. "I think that means you buddy."

Jake put his sandwich down and looked annoyed. "Man that's just great. You're too much of a wuss to have a real bachelor party so I have to go off and talk to some smart-mouthed alien about why he thinks he can kick us off our planet instead of trying to get some gorgeous stripper out of my apartment."

"Stripper?" said Nicole.

"Sorry. Exotic dancer," said Jake.

"And I'm not a wuss," said Steve.

"Yes you are," said Jake. He sat stewing for a moment then said "Well, Cynthia's not going to be happy if your wedding gets messed up because of all this and she loses out on some nice bath towels. She's liable to open up a whole case of whup-ass on the aliens." He picked up the rest of his sandwich and stood up. "Guess I better go and see what I can do before the war of the worlds breaks out. Anyone want to come with me?"

"No," said Steve.

"Yeah I forgot you're a wuss," said Jake. "Nicole? Want to come and try and take the first in focus pictures of an alien?"

"Are you kidding? That'd be great. Thanks for asking, Jake," said Nicole. She and Steve stood up to follow Jake.

"Don't mention it," said Jake as the three of them headed towards the front door of the house. "At least now I won't have to die alone if they go all Independence Day on me."

Chapter Six

It was another totally awesome summer's day as
Johnny would have described it. The spaceship sat
unchanged, glittering in the Midwest sun like a new pickup
truck. Cynthia stood watching it on the closest corner of the
front porch as Jake, Steve and Nicole came out the front
door.

"I'll be over by Cynthia giving moral support," Steve
said and he walked towards his fiancé.

"To who, me, you or her?" asked Jake and he and
Nicole continued on towards the ship, Jake munching on his
sandwich as they went.

"Where are you going, Jake?" asked Cynthia as they
walked past under the porch.

"Just going to clear up some things with the aliens,
that's all," said Jake.

"Then tell them if they ruin my wedding I'm
personally going to kick their a--" began Cynthia before Steve
reached over and covered her mouth with his hand.

"Okay. Wasn't listed on my duties of the best man
card but oh well," said Jake. He and Nicole made their way
to the pasture fence and opened the gate. Jake stopped and
popped the last bit of sandwich into his mouth then looked at
the ship and moved his head around in a circle as if to loosen
up. "No pressure at all, Jake. Just got to try to save the
human race."

Nicole brushed some crumbs off of Jake's polo shirt
then they walked over to and up the silver ramp to the top.

Jake paused and looked at Nicole for advice as to what to do next and she shrugged and Jake knocked on the door.

After a short moment a voice came from out of nowhere. *"Who is it?"* it said irritably.

"It's me," said Jake.

"Me? I don't know any me's. Go away," said the voice.

Jake narrowed his eyes, trying to look intimidating, which didn't make much sense considering the fact the door was still closed and no one inside could see him anyway. "No. Let me in. Now," he demanded.

"What are you doing?" hissed Nicole.

"Being assertive," said Jake under his breath. "That sounds like the alien from last night. He's not going to get the best of me again."

"Are you sure that's a good idea?" asked Nicole.

"No idea," said Jake.

"This is your last warning. Go away. Or else," said the voice menacingly.

"Or else what? " asked Jake.

"Or else this," said the voice.

Jake stood alertly waiting while Nicole looked on nervously but nothing happened. Jake relaxed and shrugged and at that moment he felt his feet lose all connection with the surface beneath them and he and Nicole slid ungracefully down the ramp landing at the bottom in a heap, Nicole on top of Jake.

"And stay off!" said the voice.

"Glad he didn't get the best of you," said Nicole, trying to get her bearings.

"Turned out pretty good from where I'm lying," said Jake, not altogether unpleased with he and Nicole's relative positions.

"What the heck happened anyway?" asked Nicole, her hair dangling down and tickling Jake's face.

"Don't know. All of a sudden the ramp felt like a Chicago sidewalk in winter and we both went skating," said Jake. He locked eyes with Nicole and found they were a nice shade of brown. "I think we should hold this position for a while and plan our next move."

Nicole gave Jake a sideways look then pushed herself up off his chest hard as he gasped, then stood and adjusted herself.

"Or not," said Jake, trying to catch his breath. He laid in the grass for a moment looking up at the clouds then hopped to his feet. "Let's try this again," he said. He stepped gingerly on the ramp and found it was back to normal then stomped back up it as Nicole reluctantly followed. When he got to the top he banged loudly on the door with his fist.

"*Now you're making me angry,*" said the voice. "*I told you to go away or—*"

Jake and Nicole grabbed at the sides of the ramp, expecting it to become slippery again. "Wait! Don't get all Teflon with the ramp yet. It's Jake," said Jake.

"*Jake? Just any Jake or one Jake in particular?*" asked the voice.

"Just one Jake. The Jake you talked to last night," said Jake.

"*Oh you,*" said the voice, sounding somewhat disappointed. "*The one letting the cows out of the barn.*"

Nicole gave Jake a funny look.

"Don't ask," said Jake. "Yeah that Jake," he said to the voice.

"*Just one moment,*" said the voice. There was a short pause then the door to the spaceship slid open. "*You may enter.*"

"Yeah we guessed that," said Jake. He and Nicole looked back at their friends and Steve gave them a thumbs up sign, then they walked through the arched doorway and into the ship.

Chapter Seven

The interior of the room they entered was completely empty. There was a wall that cut the ship in half with another arched door near one end of it which gave the room a half moon shape. Every surface gleamed white, and it looked like HAL would have felt right at home. Soft light emanated from strips running along the curved ceiling where it met the wall.

The door to the outside closed behind Jake and Nicole as they entered, the little yellow being from the night before standing just inside the room with a sour look on its face. "I see we've rectified our little problem," it said sarcastically. "Or was that just part of the standard Earth greeting?"

"You know for a little guy you have a pretty big mouth on you," said Jake.

"No, it is well within the universally accepted norm in proportion to my body," said the creature. "Wait here. And don't touch anything," it added before walking across the room towards the door which slid open and closed behind him as he exited.

Jake looked around him. "There's nothing to touch!" he shouted after the creature. "What do you think?" he asked Nicole.

"This is one big empty room," she said while taking a picture of it.

"Maybe they haven't unpacked yet," suggested Jake.

The door slid open again and a very large something, or more precisely someone strolled through it. The someone was tall, about seven feet or so, with a large intimidating build. His skin was soft purple in color. He had black hair with a blue tinge to it that was slicked down on his head with bushy eyebrows the same color above dark blue eyes. His nose was angular and his ears big and pointy. He wore what looked to be a kind of business suit cut in sharp angles. The jacket and pants were dark iridescent blue while the vest was dark iridescent purple. All of his fingers sported rings set with colored gem stones of some kind. Instead of a tie around his thick neck he wore a white ascot of sorts. He walked across the room in a proud, upright fashion and would have blotted out a good portion of the sun if one would have been present. Even without the eclipse Jake and Nicole were impressed and stared openly at him as he approached.

"Salutations!" said the giant in a deep dignified voice.

"Huh?" said Jake, who was wondering if this is what guards in the NBA felt like when Shaq bore down on them.

The big purple being looked down at Jake quizzically and decided to try a simpler greeting. "Hello?" he said.

"Oh yeah," said Jake, remembering finally how to communicate. "Hello. So you're--"

"Varcus Gromell at your service," said the alien, putting out a giant hand towards Jake. Jake looked at it for a long second then slowly took it and shook hands with him, his hand engulfed by the enormous mitt.

"I'm Jake," said Jake.

"Of course you are," said Varcus warmly. He looked at Nicole. "And she is?"

Jake looked at his assistant who was still staring up at Varcus and waved his hand across her eyes. "In shock I think. Her name is Nicole."

"I get that a lot I'm afraid," said Varcus, almost apologetically. "Won't you both sit down?"

Jake looked around him at the empty room. "Should we just hunker down somewhere, or..."

Varcus glanced around then looked irritated and took out a small electronic device that looked like a PED (personal electronic device) from his top jacket pocket. "My apologies. The robot should have taken care of this."

"That yellow guy's a robot?" asked Jake.

"Well to be precise a biological humanoid simulator but that's a mouthful," said Varcus, tapping on the PED.

"You might want to do something about his attitude," said Jake.

"I've tried, believe me. It seems to be hard wired in. There, that should do it," said Varcus while pressing a few more buttons on his device. A round table surrounded by three chairs rose up from the floor in the center of the room like solid turning into liquid and then back again. One of the chairs was Varcus sized, large and high backed. The other two were smaller and shaped like an upside down J, as if the being sitting in them would have to sit on the underside of the top.

Jake walked over and examined one of the crazy chairs, then looked over at Varcus. "You expect us to sit on these? Because I didn't wear my jeans with the Velcro buttocks today."

"Oops," said Varcus. "Wrong species."

"Wow. I don't even wanna know," said Jake.

"Must have hit the Hootoo button. Lovely people. Except for the constant oozing of course," explained Varcus.

"Yeah gotta hate that," said Jake.

Varcus tapped on his PED again and the two chairs flowed into something more fitting for humans and an episode of Mod Squad. "There, that's better. And let's let in a little light too shall we?" said Varcus. He pressed a couple of buttons and the round dome over their heads dissolved away. Jake and Nicole looked up, the sun beating down on their faces.

"That's a neat trick," said Jake.

"Yes, no point in being indoors on a summer's day on Earth. Please, be seated," said Varcus.

"Thanks," said Jake. He and Nicole sat down. Varcus politely waited until the two were seated then did so as well, putting his PED down on the table in front of him and leaning forward, elbows resting on the table and fingers interlaced.

Nicole held up her camera. "Would it be alright if I took some pictures of you?"

"Certainly! Go right ahead," said Varcus.

Nicole snapped a couple shots of Varcus as he sat smiling at the camera, then took a few more of the ship. She noticed she could see Steve and Cynthia on the porch now that the walls were gone and waved but they didn't seem to see her and she wondered if perhaps the walls were still there but only transparent from their perspective. When the pleasant breeze blew through her hair she decided to give up trying to figure it out and just went with it instead.

"So. What can I do for you?" asked Varcus.

It occurred to Jake that he had no idea where to begin. "Think you can get me started here?" he asked Nicole, who leaned over and whispered a suggestion into his ear. "Oh yeah, now I remember. Just what the hell do you think you're doing?"

"I beg your pardon?" said Varcus.

"That's not what I said," said Nicole.

"I liked mine better," said Jake.

"Perhaps if you could be more specific," said Varcus.

"Why are you barging into our farms handing out eviction notices to people?" demanded Jake. "And why me?"

"Ah. That," said Varcus.

"Yeah. That," said Jake.

"I'll answer the second part first. You because you were there," said Varcus.

"Meaning what?" said Jake.

"Meaning the landing spot was picked at random by a computer out of all the viable landing spots on Earth," explained Varcus. "Then I sent the robot out to find the first being he came across that he could serve notice to. It just happened to be you. So you see you were actually quite lucky."

"Boy and I'm feeling it," said Jake. "Back to the first part."

"Certainly," said Varcus. He picked up his PED, tapped a button and spoke into it. "Robot, please bring me GREEN's report," he said. "It should just be one moment. Is there anything you'd like to ask while we wait?"

"Yeah that biological human dude. What exactly is he?" asked Jake.

"He's my assistant," said Varcus. "He's able to move, think, sense and eat. And sometimes even feel I suspect, although it wasn't part of his programming."

"Almost like Rush Limbaugh," said Jake. "You know I thought he was an alien."

"Who, this Limbaugh being?" said Varcus.

"No. Well sometimes. But I meant the robot," said Jake.

"An honest mistake. Although most humanoid types I know don't go prancing around in the buff," said Varcus.

"They do it all the time here, then get paid for it," said Jake.

"You know you seem to be obsessed with strippers," said Nicole.

"He brought it up!"complained Jake.

"Hmm. Be that as it may, the robot is quite capable of experiencing everything the same way that you and I do," said Varcus.

"So if he eats a cheeseburger he's going to be one happy dude?" said Jake.

"If that's a natural reaction then yes, he might be," said Varcus.

"It is for me," said Jake.

The robot entered the room and plopped a thick report onto the table in front of Varcus.

"You ever have a cheeseburger robot?" said Jake.

"No I have not," said the robot.

"Then I guess you're not all that after all," said Jake.

51

The robot looked at Jake then shook his head and left the room.

"So why are we being evicted anyway?" said Jake.

Varcus picked up the report and held it up. It had a green cover upon which was printed in white letters *G.R.E.E.N. - Planet Earth Environmental Assessment*. "Because of this. GREEN's report on the status of the environment of the Earth."

"Who?" said Jake.

"GREEN. Galactic Representatives Encouraging Environmental Niceness," said Varcus.

"Doesn't ring a bell," said Jake.

"You know. Flying saucers. Abductions. Little green men," said Varcus.

"Oh those guys," said Nicole.

"Yes. They do independent studies of planets, testing for contamination and observing behavioral patterns to determine if a species has become a danger to their world," said Varcus.

"Is that what's with all the anal probes?" said Jake.

"No they're just mean," said Varcus. "But GREEN's report states that you humans have affected the environment of the Earth badly enough that you no longer have the ability and/or willpower to reverse it. Therefore we have no choice but to remove you from the planet before you can do any more damage."

"Can't you just help us fix things?" asked Nicole. "Surely you know what we need to do."

"Yes, but so do all of you," said Varcus. "You're just not doing it. And besides, I'm not allowed to meddle with your place in the environment."

"No you only decide if we should be allowed to stay in it or be dumped into space," said Jake.

"Dumped into space? Geebo, I'm not that cruel!" said Varcus. "No, come Monday morning you'll be transported up and moved to another world."

"Does anything good ever happen on a Monday?" said Jake.

"So where are you moving us to?" asked Nicole.

"The planet is called Gork," said Varcus.

"The names the first thing that's gonna have to go," said Jake. "What's it like?"

"Um, it's a bit of a fixer upper, but..." said Varcus, hemming and hawing.

"...but at least we'll have another home, right?" finished Nicole hopefully. "And we'll be okay there?"

"Well, estimates are that eighty-three percent of you will be dead within the first year but you could surprise us," said Varcus.

"Glad you're not that cruel," said Jake.

"You've left us with no choice I'm afraid. You already have the Earth teetering on the brink of environmental disaster. We can't very well leave you here so you can shove it over the edge," said Varcus.

"I don't suppose you could just go away for a year or two and give us a chance to straighten things up," said Jake.

"It wouldn't help. Like I said, according to the report you've passed the point where your species can or will put things to right. Believe me, I'm not happy about it either. I've become quite fond of you humans," said Varcus.

"Obviously," said Jake.

"No really," said Varcus. "I've spent almost a million years with you people, helping you out, watching over you. And now I have to come here and do this."

"Exactly what do you mean by helping us out?" said Nicole.

"Let me explain," said Varcus. "You see I'm sort of a case worker for fledgling sentient races. One of my duties is to give them a little assistance whenever they hit a wall in their development. Take Earth for example. I taught your people how to use fire, how to make a wheel, how to fish, how to ride horses--"

"Did we figure anything out on our own?" said Nicole.

"Well, you did start hitting each other over the head with rocks without my help," said Varcus brightly.

"Great. Did you teach us about anything cool or fun?" said Jake.

Varcus thought for a moment. "I did teach you how to make alcohol. You were all getting so tense, fighting and killing one another all the time. I thought it might calm you down a bit. Give you a way to unwind."

"Did it help?" asked Jake.

"No," said Varcus sadly. "You just killed one another and went home and got drunk and celebrated. Then you woke up all hung over and grouchy so you went out and killed each other some more."

"That sounds like us," said Nicole. "You know, Varcus, I have to say you look pretty good for someone who's a million years old."

"Thank you, but I'm only one-hundred and twelve," said Varcus. "I didn't hang around while you evolved if that's what you're asking. I traveled forward through time."

"You can time travel too?" said Nicole.

"It's really not that difficult. Anyone can do it. Even you," said Varcus.

"I seriously doubt that," said Nicole.

"No really. I'll prove it to you. Close your eyes and hold very still and concentrate hard about something," said Varcus.

"Alright," said Nicole. She closed her eyes and thought very hard about clocks, but got sidetracked by trying to decide between analog and digital.

Varcus sat watching her then said "You see? You just went forward in time."

Nicole opened her eyes. "Very funny."

"It breaks the ice at parties. Anyway we've just discovered how to go ahead faster. It's going back in time that no one's figured out yet," said Varcus.

"If we're done with the bar tricks can we get back to business before the moving vans arrive?" said Jake.

"Of course," said Varcus. "But I don't know what else I can tell you. My hands are tied. Planets that can sustain life are a rare and precious thing and it's everyone's duty to protect them, and the Earth is one of the nicer worlds in the galaxy. I'm not sure I would leave you here even if I could. As it is I have to abide by the guidelines set down by the Galactic Council."

"So what am I supposed to do now? Go back and tell everyone there's no hope and they might as well start packing their Samsonites?" said Jake.

Varcus stood and picked up his PED. "Tell them what I told you. Just the facts."

"Yeah that should go over big," said Jake. He and Nicole stood up and they and Varcus headed towards the ramp. Varcus tapped on the PED and the door to the outside reappeared and opened. Nicole went through the door then looked back and saw that the walls of the ship were indeed still there from the outside. Curious, she reached out with her hand and felt metal against her fingers, then stuck her head back inside. The walls were still invisible from the interior, but when she tried to put her hand through them found she could not. She came to the conclusion that the walls were like a one way mirror that at the same time somehow let sunlight and air through them.

Varcus and Jake stood watching Nicole, both amused by her experimentation. Jake waited until she was finished and was about to leave when he remembered something and stopped and turned back to face Varcus. "Oh, by the way, Cynthia said if you mess up her wedding she's going to kick your--" he began.

"Cynthia?" asked Varcus.

"The gal who owns the farm the computer decided to park you in," said Jake.

"Oh. Well you can assure her that I've taken measures not to affect the day to day lives of you humans," said Varcus.

"Yeah like moving us off the planet won't mess up our routines," said Jake. He started to turn away again but had yet another thought. "Hey these measures of yours. They wouldn't have anything to do with the fact that we can't get any authority types to come here and help us out would they?"

"That would be me yes," said Varcus. "Things go much smoother this way. There's nothing more counter-productive than listening to a room full of bureaucrats argue and point fingers at one another. So I just see to it that they choose to stay away. And that they don't suddenly think that lobbing a nuclear missile or two at me would be a really neat idea."

"And is that why the yard isn't full of reporters and gawkers interviewing bovine witnesses?" asked Jake.

"That too yes. Just a little nothing to see here move along vibe," said Varcus.

"Must be the same thing Paris Hilton puts out but in reverse," said Jake. "I trust you do plan to let the rest of the planet in on what's going on eventually so they can at least feed the fish before they go."

"Don't worry. Everyone will know," said Varcus. "In fact, you might want to catch the broadcast yourself. Just turn on the television tomorrow at noon your time."

"What channel?" said Jake.

"All of them," said Varcus. "Everything will be explained."

"Good. And no offense but I hope everyone leaves you with a big pile of dirty dishes," said Jake. He put his hand up in goodbye then exited the spaceship and the door closed behind him. Varcus watched him go through the transparent wall and shook his head sadly and sighed.

"Nice beings. Doesn't get much tougher than that," he said somberly, then clapped his hands. "Well, let's see what's on TV."

Chapter Eight

The sun was down, the birds had all gone to bed and the wedding rehearsal dinner was in full swing in the yard behind the farmhouse about fifty yards away from but strategically out of sight of the alien ship. Two picnic tables were covered with checkered cloths, fried chicken, mashed potatoes, baked beans and wedding party members and family. Jake and Nicole sat at one of the tables with Steve, his parents James and Carolyn, and Cynthia and her grandfather Pete. Mark, Craig, Tommy and the two bridesmaids, Paula and Julia, sat at the other table. Jake gnawed hungrily on a chicken leg, having worked up quite an appetite during rehearsal trying to walk down the aisle in a straight line without going too fast or too slow while wondering what the hell to do about the minor fact that they were well on their way to becoming extra terrestrials.

"Good eats, Cynthia," said Jake between bites. "You're a lucky man Steve."

"Yes I am," said Steve, smiling at his fiancé.

"You must be too, Jake," said Pete, a kindly looking elderly gentleman. Pete had the happy and sad duty of standing in at the wedding for Cynthia's parents who had died in an automobile accident two years previous. "How many people get to meet a real live alien?"

"About ten a month if you believe the Weekly World News," said Nicole.

"You read that thing?" asked Jake.

"Never," said Nicole, failing to look him in the eye.

"Sure," said Jake.

"So tell us all about this spaceman," said Pete.

"Well, his name is Varcus and--" began Jake.

"No alien talk during the rehearsal dinner please!" interrupted Cynthia curtly, still clinging desperately to the hope that she could manage a normal wedding.

"Now, Cynthia," said Carolyn. "Your grandfather has the right to know what's going on."

"I'm curious myself," said James. "I'd like to know if that ship coming to Earth is going to affect the stock market."

"Oh yeah. It's gonna affect it alright," said Jake.

"Well do you think I should buy or sell?" asked James.

"Won't make a whole lot of difference either way I'm thinking," said Jake.

"So is this Varcus more like an ET alien or a Terminator alien?" asked Pete.

"The Terminator was a robot Granddad," said Cynthia.

"Yeah but Varcus has one of those too and it's got almost as bad an attitude as Arnold," said Jake.

"Why are they here anyway?" Cynthia asked. "And don't tell me you don't know. I can tell you guys are hiding something."

"They gave you a scroll of some kind didn't they?" asked Tommy from the next table.

"Yeah Steve won't talk about it," complained Mark.

"Maybe you will," purred Paula, who had a tendency to purr every time she wanted something from a male and then usually got it.

"Um," said Jake. "You know Steve is the one who actually read the scroll. You should probably ask him about it."

"Yeah but you're the Representative," argued Steve.

"Yeah but you're the fiancé," countered Jake. "You're the one who's not supposed to be keeping secrets. I'm single. I can be as covert as I want."

"Representative? Representative of what?" asked Carolyn.

"What secrets? What's going on?" asked Pete.

Jake sensed that the crowd was beginning to grow ugly, at least as ugly as a wedding party could get and he looked over at Nicole for help.

"Maybe you should just tell them," said Nicole. "They're going to find out tomorrow anyway."

"You sure that's a good idea?" said Jake.

"Tell us what, Jake?" demanded Cynthia.

Everyone sat staring at Jake who sighed and rubbed his head. "Okay. If you say so," said Jake. "Let's see. How can I put this? Cynthia, are you and Steve planning on having kids?"

"Not right this minute," said Cynthia. "So if that's why that spaceship is here you can go tell them we plan to wait and they can leave and come back later."

"And what do you two plan on using? Cloth or disposables?" asked Jake.

Steve and Cynthia looked at one another and then back at Jake. "Are you kidding?" said Cynthia. "Have you ever smelled those things?"

Jake leaned back on the picnic bench. "I rest my case."

"That's why the alien is here?" Cynthia said to Steve. "Because you and I don't want to wash poopy diapers?"

"Basically yeah," said Steve.

Cynthia looked at Nicole to see if she too had suddenly gone crazy along with the males but she just shrugged and nodded her head. "I don't get it," said Cynthia.

"Look, the alien says we've dirtied up the Earth so he's kicking us all off of it and moving us to the planet Gork," said Jake.

"Gork? What kind of a name is that for a planet?" asked Pete, somehow missing the larger problem.

"Well I doubt if anyone out in the rest of the universe is real impressed with *Earth* either," said Jake.

"Well can we rename it?" asked Tommy.

"Yes. No. Maybe. I don't know," said Jake. "The point is come Monday morning we're scheduled to be evicted."

"Monday?!" screeched Cynthia.

"Yeah," said Jake.

"They can't move us on Monday!" said Cynthia.

"Would Tuesday be a whole lot better?" said Jake.

Cynthia pouted. "My honeymoon..." she said sniffily.

"I know how you feel but--" said Jake.

"We were going to the Wisconsin Dells!" snapped Cynthia angrily.

"Hey it could be worse," said Jake.

"How could it possibly be any worse?" said Cynthia.

"At least you're here with your friends and family," said Jake. "Imagine the people sitting around the dinner table with Al Gore when he finds out. He's never gonna stop saying I told you so."

Cynthia got up from the table. "I'm going to go and have a talk with him," she said determinedly.

Jake stood up quickly and moved to intercept. "No, no, no, no. That's not a good idea at all."

"Why not?" said Cynthia.

"Because, Cynthia, you're a great gal who's engaged to my best friend but you go stomping over to that space ship all angry and worked up and Varcus is liable to say The heck with this and just take off and disintegrate the planet," said Jake. "And you guys haven't even cut the cake yet."

Cynthia stomped her feet, which had little effect in the soft grass. "Well what am I supposed to do then?" she asked.

"Go to bed tonight and get up tomorrow and marry that man over there," said Jake. "Then blame him for the whole thing."

Cynthia sat back down. "Fine. But you keep an eye on that alien."

"Gonna be hard to do tomorrow while I'm making sure you two get hitched," said Jake.

"Maybe you should just invite him to the wedding then," suggested Pete.

"Yeah that's all I need," said Cynthia.

Jake thought about it for a moment. "You know that's not a bad idea."

"What?" asked Steve.

"Varcus. Inviting him to your wedding," said Jake.

"Are you out of your mind?" asked Cynthia.

"Probably," said Jake. "I do believe I've been talking to aliens and robots lately. Look, this is important, Cynthia. Varcus really needs to come to your wedding."

"No way, Jake. I'm not going to have some little green man getting drunk and eating the DJ," said Cynthia.

"He's purple, not green. Big too. The DJ would probably only be a light snack for him," said Jake. "Steve, you know how you're always going on about the planet being doomed? Well here's your chance to try and do something about it."

"I thought the planet was going to be fine once we're gone and it's us that's in trouble," said Steve.

"Picky picky," said Jake.

"So how is inviting the alien to my wedding going to help?" said Steve.

"No clue," said Jake. "Maybe give me some time to schmooze him? You know how good I am at that. Besides, does anybody here have any better ideas?"

Everyone looked at each other, which made Tommy, Mark and Craig happy because it gave them a legitimate excuse to stare at Paula some more.

"Then it's settled. I'll go over there right now and talk to him," said Jake. "Hey, Steve, why don't you come with me and do the invite."

"Me? Did you forget I'm a wuss already?" complained Steve.

"Time to man-up," said Jake. "Come on, it'd be more sincere if you do it. Otherwise he might think I'm just trying to get him out of the ship so we can hit him with something heavy."

Steve got up from the table. "That might not be a bad idea. What about Cynthia?"

Cynthia glared angrily at Steve. "You really want me coming along?" she said through gritted teeth.

"Uh, maybe not," said Steve.

"Yeah, the whole sincerity thing would kinda fly out the window," said Jake. "Let's go," he said, and he and Steve walked around the corner of the house towards the pasture.

Chapter Nine

"You know, you're not getting my marriage off on the right foot Jake," said Steve as they approached the ship.

"Yeah, but someday you can tell the grandkids all about the day the alien danced with their grandmother," said Jake.

"Our wedding video's are gonna end up on You Tube," said Steve. He and Jake walked up the ramp and Jake knocked on the door.

"Hopefully we won't get the butler," said Jake.

A short minute later the door opened and Varcus stood before them wearing a long deep blue puffy robe over silky blue pajamas, his feet nuzzled by big fuzzy slippers in the shape of some reptilian alien animal. In his hand was a glass filled with green glowing liquid replete with swizzle stick. In the background Jake could hear the sound of a television.

"Jake! Good to see you again so soon," said Varcus happily.

"I hope we didn't wake you," said Jake.

"Oh no," said Varcus. "I was just watching some TV and unwinding with a nightcap. What can I do for you?"

"Well I told my man Steve here all about you and he insisted on coming over and meeting you," said Jake. He looked at Steve who stood staring at Varcus and Jake poked him in the ribs with his elbow. "Isn't that right, Steve?"

"Yes! Yes I did," said Steve, recovering nicely. "I was wondering if you'd like to come to my wedding tomorrow."

"He's marrying Cynthia," said Jake.

"Really? I'm a bit surprised you'd want me there all things considered," said Varcus.

"Well he thought you might be a little lonely out here," said Jake. "Besides, Steve's one of those save the planet kind of guys too so he kind of knows where you're coming from."

Steve thought about pointing out that he actually had no idea where Varcus had come from but decided to keep quiet about it.

"Hmm," said Varcus thoughtfully. "This is very unusual. Oh what the heck. I've never been to an Earth wedding before. It might be fun. I'd be honored to attend."

"Great!" enthused Steve despite thinking it wasn't all that great at all.

"You know I never asked if you had any friends along in there," said Jake.

"No just me and the robot," said Varcus. "Oh, and the thousands of automated transport ships orbiting your planet of course."

"Yeah can't forget those," said Jake.

The robot walked up behind Varcus. "You asked me to remind you to change the channel when it's time for *Law and Order?*" he asked in an annoyed tone.

"I did. Switch it for me please," said Varcus.

"Yes, your highnessness," said the robot sarcastically, then moved off to do so.

Varcus sighed. "He gets more surly every day. His model has always been a bit quirky."

"So I noticed," said Jake. "Would it help if you brought him along tomorrow?"

"Only if I wanted to be miserable. He does need to get out of the ship though. I think he's getting a bit stir crazy," said Varcus.

"Maybe we could find someone to show him around while you're at the wedding," said Jake.

"That would be most kind of you. And the data he collects would be very valuable. You know, preserving a lost culture," said Varcus.

Jake and Steve looked at Varcus with a why did you have to go and say a thing like that sort of look.

"Oops," said Varcus. "Sorry. Don't want to put a damper on things do we? What time should we be ready?"

"One o'clock okay?" said Jake. "Or will that get in the way of your broadcast?"

"No I tend to keep it brief. Most species have such a short attention span these days," said Varcus. "Of course I will miss the Cubs game but..."

"You like baseball huh?" said Jake. "So what do you watch the games on? You got a plasma in there?"

Varcus stepped aside. "See for yourself."

Jake and Steve stuck their heads into the spaceship and looked. There was now a big comfortable looking recliner formed out of the floor facing the center wall the entirety of which was acting as an extremely big high-def TV.

"Wow," said Jake enviously. "Now that's what I want for the Bears games."

"Packers games," said Steve.

Jake and Steve withdrew their heads from the room. "Whatever," said Jake. "Guess we'll see you tomorrow then Varcus."

"I look forward to it," said Varcus. "And thanks again for inviting me."

"No problem. Good night," said Steve.

Varcus waved goodbye and closed the door and Jake and Steve walked back down the ramp.

"Nice job," said Jake. "You know you did pretty well for your first time talking to an alien."

"I just pretended it was a dream without Jessica," said Steve. He looked up at the stars. "Hey I wonder if you can see Gork's sun from here."

"Look for the ugliest ball of gas you can find and that'll probably be it," said Jake.

"They all kind of look alike," said Steve. "But I do see a UFO."

"Ha ha. You said that last night too and look what happened," said Jake. "Maybe if you'd stop looking up all the time you'd stop attracting aliens."

"Too late," said Steve.

Jake put his head back and scanned the night sky and his shoulders slumped. "Now look what you've done," he said, staring at the brightly lit spacecraft descending towards them. "What is this place, L.A.X. for aliens?"

"We don't have to invite them to my wedding too do we?" asked Steve.

They watched the new ship glide towards the Earth. It was elongated, shaped like a classic rocket ship out of the Buck Rogers era and while it wasn't much larger than Varcus' craft it was certainly a lot gaudier, gold in color and covered with thousands of multicolored lights blinking on and off in eye pleasing patterns. Antennae, radar dishes and indiscernible apparatuses poked out in every direction from the hull. Moving spotlights shone both into the air and onto the Earth as it approached. As it neared the ground spider-like landing gear unfolded out of bays on the ship's bottom and the vessel glided to a landing about thirty yards or so away from Varcus'. A short ramp with gold posts and velvet ropes for railings unfolded in impressive fashion under a door in the side of the craft over which unrolled a red carpet. The door slid open and a humanoid stepped out with a flourish, his four hands on his hips, white spotlights shining down on him from the top of the ship.

The new alien could have easily passed for a human if it were not for his two extra limbs. His facial features were chiseled, handsome in a he-man sort of way, almost like a statue. He stood well over six feet tall, broad shouldered, appearing to be a bit taller due to the pointy gold metal helmet perched on his head. He wore a silky red uniform replete with two rows of gold buttons running up and down the front. Each of the hands at the end of his four arms were covered in blue leather looking gloves while his feet sported matching boots. A wide gold belt wrapped around his waist with several small packs and devices attached to it. A white cape trimmed with gold hung on his bag and rustled in the soft evening breeze. All in all he looked like a cross between Superman and Sergeant Peppers.

"Greetings people of Earth!" the alien said loudly, his voice booming around the farm. "I bring you good tidings of

70

cheeses and alternative living arrangements. Is there one among you who can speak on your behalf?"

"Not it," said Jake and he gently pushed Steve towards the alien. "It's your turn to play Representative."

Steve reluctantly walked over to the newcomer. "Hail, citizen!" said the alien in greeting while snapping off a crisp four handed salute.

"Uh, hail," said Steve, looking down at his own two hands and wondering if and how he was expected to salute back. "I'm Steve."

"Here is some cheese," said the alien, taking a chunk of a cheese-like substance from one of his packs and handing it to Steve who looked at it like he'd been handed a live grenade. "Now that I have proven my friendship we can begin negotiations. Are you the Representative?"

Steve shook his head no and pointed over at Jake.

"Damn!" said Jake. He sighed and made his way over as Steve happily retreated to Cynthia who along with the rest of the wedding party had come around the side of the house to find out what all the racket was about. "Jake Williams, Representative, who the hell are you, what do you want and what did we do now?"

"You sound agitated, citizen," said the alien. "Here, take this cheese and eat it. It will calm you," he said, taking another piece from his pack and trying to hand it to Jake.

"I'm not taking anything from you," said Jake. "For all I know that's some sort of dairy based alien lawsuit."

"Hmm. You seem suspicious of the cheese. That contradicts my brief studies of the area," said the alien.

"I'm only *visiting* Wisconsin," said Jake.

"Ah. That would explain the paradox," said the alien. "Then I will try to proceed as best I can without a peace offering. But without the mutual trust that comes with the gift of coagulated animal by-products to an inferior culture I am dubious of my chances of success."

"Yeah, well we'll just have to muddle along then won't we?" said Jake. "Now I'd appreciate it if you'd just tell me who you are and what you want because we're chock full of aliens right now and I'm not really sure we need another."

"I appreciate your get down to businessness and will do so also," said the alien. "I am Larry," he said, sticking his enormous chin out as if for emphasis.

"Larry?" said Jake. "Your name is Larry?"

"Yes. I'm glad that you're able to understand," said Larry. "I've come to your world to save you and your people."

"An alien named Larry is here to save us?" said Jake.

"Very good human," said Larry. "You're much more intelligent than many of your entertainments have led me to believe. Although admittedly the genius of your Rob Schneider cannot be denied."

Varcus, still wearing his robe and fuzzy lizard slippers, hurried over to Jake and Larry. "Jake, don't listen to a thing that man says. He cannot be trusted."

"Ouch. It hurts to hear you say that, Varcus," said Larry.

"You two know each other?" said Jake. "I thought this was supposed to be a big universe."

"Not big enough for me to stop bumping into him," said Varcus. "I don't know what harebrained scheme he's cooked up this time but I beg you not to talk to him."

"Well if you're going to beg..." said Jake.

"Good. So you'll steer clear of him then?" said Varcus.

"Not for a moment. Well these moments anyway," said Jake. "Later on I might go running and screaming in the opposite direction though."

"But why?" asked Varcus.

"I listened to you didn't I? It's only fair I do the same for Larry before I start wishing he never landed here like I do with you," said Jake.

"Fine, be that way. I can't stop you. Just please don't sign anything," said Varcus.

"I'll wait until I have an attorney present," said Jake, then feigned surprise and pointed over at Steve. "Oh look, there's one over there!"

"Joke if you want. You've been warned," warned Varcus. He turned and headed back to his ship and Larry motioned towards his.

"Perhaps it would be more private if we adjourn to the privacy of my space craft where we might enjoy a modicum of uh, privacy," said Larry.

"Why not? The man says I can't trust you so I'm bound to just walk inside your ship like an idiot," said Jake. "Lead the way, Larry."

Chapter Ten

The inside of Larry's ship looked like a cheap honeymoon suite. A huge heart shaped bed covered by a red fur spread sat on a raised platform against one wall under a shining disco ball. A hot tub bubbled over by the other wall, a Cupid fountain tinkling into it. Furniture was scattered around the room, the couches and chairs covered in crushed velvet and animal print furs. Lava lamps bubbled on every end table and black velvet paintings that looked like they were from Mexico hung on the walls.

"You know normally if a guy invited me into his bedroom I might be a little leery but the gay men I know have better taste than this," said Jake.

"The interior of my ship was scientifically designed to make the fairer and more shoe oriented citizens go weak in the knees upon entering its confines," said Larry.

"And it works does it?" asked Jake doubtfully.

"Yes. With the magnitude of my attractiveness I'm not sure it's really necessary but you can't be too careful when it comes to chicks," said Larry. He took out his PED, showing he too was a member of the growing number of species in the galaxy who couldn't tie their shoes without one and pressed a button and two paintings swung out of the way revealing a fully stocked bar. "Martini?"

"Thanks but I had some drinks in me when I ran into Varcus' robot last night and we all know how that turned out for the Earth," said Jake.

"Then I'll join you in your abstinence," said Larry. "Please be seated and we'll speak about how I, Larry, will gallantly save your entire race."

Jake and Larry sat down. "Are you trying to tell me you can stop Varcus from evicting us from the Earth?" asked Jake, managing to sound hopeful and doubtful at the same time.

"Sorry, that I can't gallantly do," said Larry.

"Then why am I sitting here on a fake zebra fur loveseat?" said Jake, standing up to leave.

"Because what I can gallantly do is give your people a superior planet on which to hang their backwards and sideways worn hats," said Larry. "Have you ever been to Gork?"

"Nope, haven't built up enough frequent flier miles yet. But I was in Detroit once," said Jake.

"Ah, Detroit. City of muscle cars and flying bullets," said Larry. "I lost one wallet and four watches there one day."

"Yeah, that'd be the one," said Jake.

"Gork is worse," said Larry.

Jake sat back down. "Wow," he said, clearly impressed. "You've got my attention. So what's the deal? Do you have a planet in the Caribbean sector of space that just happens to be vacant?"

Larry tapped on his PED and the ship dissolved around them and he and Jake and the zebra furniture were suddenly on a beautiful beach covered with alien palm trees.

Jake surveyed his surroundings as a warm ocean breeze blew through his hair. The sky above him was rose colored and the water was turquoise, gold specks of light glittering upon it. Two suns, one slightly larger than the other, were just setting on the horizon. Exotic colorful birds flew through the sky.

"This is the planet Aurora, home of sandy beaches and rum every night," said Larry. "At least there would be rum if anybody lived there. What do you think?"

"I've seen better," said Jake as the waves lapped gently against the white sand shore near his feet.

"Sure you have," said Larry.

"If it's so great then why is it empty?" asked Jake.

"It's not empty," said Larry. "Many creatures frolic upon its surface. But none of them have bothered to evolve into something that would put up advertising."

"Then why hasn't someone colonized it?" asked Jake.

"You've seen too many of your 2d movies," said Larry. "Real life colonization is most complicated and involves oodles of money and even more paperwork. Most species don't bother and just stay at home."

"So why would it be worth it for us then?" asked Jake.

"Because I, Larry, am involved," said Larry.

"That's not an answer," said Jake. "It sounds more like an impediment."

"Then because it's my planet," said Larry. "And I can do what I want with it."

"How did you end up with your own planet?" asked Jake.

"Lawsuit," said Larry. "I slipped on a Walada peel in a Mega Mart and fell. With gross negligence comes gross settlements."

"So then what's the catch?" asked Jake.

Larry tapped on the PED and the scene disappeared, much to Jake's disappointment.

"There is nothing to catch," said Larry. "You have need of a planet to populate and I have an empty one that's beginning to gather dust. It would be a most equitable arrangement for both of us."

"But why us in particular?" said Jake. "I mean, why humans and our inferior culture?"

"You mean besides the fact you're the only species about to be ejected from their planet right now?" asked Larry.

"Yes, besides that," said Jake.

"Pizza," said Larry.

"Pizza?" asked Jake.

"Yes. In spite of your backwardsness your people have created the perfect food," said Larry. "It's round. And tomatoey. And herby. And, and, and--"

"Cheesy?" said Jake.

"Ah. So you understand cheese after all," said Larry. "Yes, it is cheesy as well. Great gooey stringy golden brown gobs of cheese melting on my tongue and burning the roof of my mouth."

"And that's it? We have pizza so that makes us your immigrants of choice?" said Jake.

"Could there be a better yardstick by which to measure a species worthiness?" asked Larry.

"I guess it'd rate pretty high on who I'd want to co-habitate with," said Jake. "So we bring the pizza and you move us to this planet of yours. What's it called again? Aldora?"

"Aurora. Like those Northern Lights that I could stare at for hours but don't because they only happen where it's cold," said Larry.

"Well it's got Gork's name beat by a mile, that's for sure," said Jake.

"So should I draw up the papers so we can legalize your movement?" said Larry.

"Sure, draw 'em up," said Jake.

"Most excellent!" said Larry happily.

"But I'm not signing them," said Jake.

"You're not?" said Larry, not so happily.

"No. At least not yet," said Jake.

"But why? Either you make the deal and take your pizza to paradise or you don't and you take it to Gork where it will be most melancholy," said Larry.

Jake stood up. "Because I never sign anything without talking to my clients first."

"You're going to talk to all the humans?" said Larry. "I must tell you this is a limited time offer. It expires in about one week, not one century."

"I can't talk to everyone, but I can talk to a few people I know," said Jake. "They'll probably just tell me it's up to me, but at least I'll have asked. Besides, I'd still rather find a way for everyone to stay here on Earth."

Larry stood and put all four of his hands up in front of him in a quadruple fine sort of gesture. "No problem, I understand. I do not wish to pressurize you. Take as much of your time as you want. Just don't take any more of it than that."

"Good.. I'll get back to you," said Jake. He and Larry walked towards the door and stopped at the exit. "So how did you get a planet in a lawsuit? It sounds a wee bit excessive to me for simply falling down."

"I didn't just fall down. I twisted my ankle," said Larry.

"And?" said Jake.

"It hurt like the dickens," said Larry.

"And they awarded you a planet for that?" asked Jake.

"My people were the only species with lawyers at the time. Everyone else had outlawed and/or executed theirs," said Larry. "Since then we've done the same."

"So humans are the only civilized race left in the galaxy with attorneys?" said Jake.

"No, that would be a contradiction in terms," said Larry. He pushed the open button next to the door and it opened, which surprised no one. "Perhaps we could meet again and talk some more tomorrow. I would welcome a healthy debate on the merits of pepperoni versus Italian sausage."

"I'm going to be pretty busy tomorrow. I sort of have a wedding to be in," said Jake, wondering immediately if it had been a good idea to bring it up.

"A wedding?" said Larry excitedly. "I happen to love weddings as long as I'm not expected to vow anything."

"Is that a fact?" said Jake, sure now it *had* been a bad idea and hoping to just get out of the ship before the conversation finished going where it seemed to be heading.

"Yes. There are always females there, full of desire to find a mate after watching a member of their chromosome club become legally attached," said Larry. He looked at Jake with an attempt at puppy dog eyes, which in a roundabout way worked because it creeped Jake out so bad he would've done anything to make him stop.

"I know Cynthia's gonna kill me for this, but we already invited your neighbor alien to the wedding so I guess I should invite you too," said Jake.

"Why thank you. You certainly didn't need to do that," said Larry, feigning surprise.

"Well I didn't want to see you start crying either," said Jake. "Be ready at one o'clock and meet up with Varcus. You two can go together. That should annoy him."

Jake waved goodbye and exited the ship. Outside he walked over towards Steve and the rest of the wedding party who were slowly heading towards the house, bored already with the new alien.

"So is he coming to my wedding?" said Steve who'd been patiently waiting to ask that question.

"You know he is," said Jake.

"Great. Are you going to tell Cynthia?" said Steve.

"No you are, but she'll blame me like always," said Jake.

"That seems fair," said Steve. "You coming inside?"

Jake looked over at Nicole who was standing off by herself taking pictures of Larry's ship. "Yeah in just a minute."

Steve went inside the house and Jake walked over to Nicole. "So who's the new guy?" she asked.

"Just some real estate agent. He has some beach front property he thought we might be interested in opening a pizza parlor on. I told him we'd think about it," said Jake.

"If you say so," said Nicole. "You know I'd love to see the inside of his ship too."

"Just don't go without a chaperone. With those four arms of his I don't think you'd make it out of that love pit unmolested," said Jake.

"Thanks for the warning." Nicole took one last picture and put her camera in her shirt pocket. "So what are you going to do now?" she asked.

"Probably go inside and get some sleep. You?" said Jake.

"I guess I'll head back over to the bed and breakfast. I hate to though. I don't know what I might miss," said Nicole.

"You could stay with me," said Jake.

Nicole looked at Jake in surprise.

"With us!" said Jake quickly. "Us meaning everyone in there. Not with me, me. In the farmhouse I mean. Well I'd be in there too. You know, just not..."

Nicole was still studying Jake quizzically so he continued his clarification.

"Plenty of space. Lots of bedrooms. Big house," said Jake.

"That's what I thought you meant," said Nicole.

"Uh-huh," said Jake.

They stood awkwardly silent for a moment looking everywhere but at one another.

"What?!" yelled Cynthia angrily from inside the house. "Steve..."

"What was that all about?" asked Nicole, startled.

"That'd be all about me," said Jake. "Come on, we better get inside before Steve ends up with a black eye for the wedding pictures."

Chapter Eleven

"Yeah, ma, I know. I'm doing everything I can," said Jake into his cell phone. "No I don't know what the weather is like on Gork this time of year. I know it makes packing difficult but I don't know if we get to bring anything anyway. No I don't think we're all going to be running around naked. Just watch the broadcast. And let dad have a drink if he wants one. In fact let him have two. Look, ma, I gotta go. Yeah I'll be sure and tell the alien that. Bye mom. Love you too. Bye. Bye." Jake hung up the phone and put it in his tux pocket.

"What are you supposed to tell Varcus?" asked Steve as he paced nervously back and forth in the waiting room of the church.

"Dad needs a firm mattress," said Jake.

"Hey is this is it?" asked Craig, pointing at the TV.

Jake, Steve and Mark gathered around the television. The screen was black, except for some green letters that said *A message to all Earthlings*.

"Yeah, this might be it. Nice job figuring that out, Craig," said Steve condescendingly.

"Thanks," said Craig.

The TV screen changed. Varcus sat at a table in the room on his ship where he had met with Jake and Nicole. He wore a shiny blue suit in the style of his planet with a white vest and light blue ascot. He stared blankly at the camera, smiling. "Is this thing on?" he said finally. "Are we live? Okay. Hello people of Earth! My name is Varcus Gromell and I come from the planet Vandor. Recently the Galactic

Council received a report--" Varcus stopped and looked around him then addressed someone off camera. "Robot! Where is the report? I thought I told you to have it here on the table for the broadcast! Yes I can see it's not here, where is it? Never mind, it's too late now. We'll talk about it later." He turned back to the camera. "Well I have it here somewhere. Anyway, it's from the independent environmental testing organization known as GREEN and simply put their conclusion is that you humans have pushed the Earth to the brink of environmental disaster to the point where you no longer have the knowledge and desire to reverse what you have done. Therefore to protect the planet from further harm you are to be evicted from it Monday morning, nine a.m. U.S. Central Time."

"So it's true," said Mark. "I thought maybe you guys were pulling some elaborate practical joke."

"We still could be," said Steve.

"Not anymore. It's on TV so it must be true," said Craig.

"Boy are you the perfect American," said Jake.

Varcus continued. "You will all be, in your Earth cultural terms, beamed up to one of thousands of transport ships now in orbit around your planet then relocated to your new home on the planet Gork in the Keeselhorse System. You may bring with you only what you can carry. Weapons and explosives are not allowed, although since there is a soothing pacifist ray currently aimed at your planet you wouldn't think to bring them anyway but I thought I'd mention it just in case."

"Good thing it's not football season," said Jake. "They'd probably have to play touch."

"I heard on the news that the crime rate over the last couple of days was at a new all time low," said Mark. "Zero. All the wars have come to a screeching halt too."

"Well, something good came out of all this anyway," said Steve.

"Also you will not be allowed to bring live animals," said Varcus. "Your pets will be well taken care of after you depart and we wouldn't want to destroy the eco system on Gork, such as it is, with a stray gerbil or goldfish now would we? The seven or so billion of you should be quite enough of a shock to the poor planet. A short film will follow this announcement giving you all the information you'll need to prepare for the move to your new home. It should be noted that for the first thirty days of your life on Gork there will also be a pacifist ray pointed at that planet so you'll have to wait before you can begin to throw rocks and spears at one other. That's about it from me. It's been nice talking to you. Enjoy the film and have a great and happy Earth day!"

Varcus sat smiling at the camera for a moment.

"Okay, start the film," said Varcus from the corner of his mouth.

Varcus remained smiling stiffly at the camera. "Look, you stupid robot just start the drooging film before I--"

The picture on the TV changed to a cheesy screen that said *You and your big move to Gork!* as equally cheesy and happy music played. It immediately reminded Jake of sleeping through all the similarly styled films he was supposed to be watching in high school. The picture changed again and a crude cartoon of a human stood in the middle of his living room scratching his head as a voice over began.

"So you and your people are moving to Gork," said the narrator. "Well, good for you. You probably have many questions, and I'm here to help. Let's ask Sam here, a typical human, what he thinks he needs to know."

"You've got to be kidding me," said Jake.

The cartoon Sam looked at the camera. "Well I guess first I'd like to know what the heck I should I bring with me!"

"Why that's entirely up to you, Sam," said the narrator happily. "You could bring your golf clubs, blender, pink flamingo, teddy bear, grandfather clock, Rice Krispy bars, CD collection, why even the kitchen sink!" he said, the cartoon film piling all the items onto Sam as he spoke. "But keep in mind since there's no electricity on Gork at the moment you may just want to bring some clothes and a good book. And maybe that teddy bear."

"I would like to bring some clothes," said Sam. "but what's the weather like on Gork?"

"Well, If you live in a warm climate you're going to like it on Gork!" said the narrator enthusiastically. "And if you live in a cold one you'll never have to worry about those freezing winters again! The average temperature on Gork is a balmy one-hundred and six degrees Fahrenheit!"

"Gee, it sounds better than a day at the beach!" said Sam excitedly.

"Okay, Sam's an idiot," said Steve.

"Well they did say he was a typical human," said Jake.

"When you arrive on Gork you'll find temporary shelters, water and rations to last six Gorkian months. So you'll have everything you'll need to get started!" said the narrator. "But don't forget, one day on Gork is only about nine Earth hours long so you'll have to get busy finding those alternative food sources right away. Just think how short your work day will be!"

"Sounds great! Can I go right now?" said Sam.

The cheesy music swelled to a happy conclusion as the film winded down.

"Be patient, Sam," said the narrator. "The big day will come soon enough. We hope the rest of you humans are now as excited as Sam about your big move to the planet Gork. We look forward to watching you scratch and claw to tame this wild and vibrant planet. Thanks for watching and have a great and happy Earth day!"

The screen went blank then switched back to regular programming.

"I don't know about the rest of you but somehow I don't feel a whole lot better," said Steve.

"Yeah, if it wasn't for that ray I'd say a general state of panic would have set in just about now," said Jake. "Hey I forgot to ask. Did you ever find anyone to baby sit Varcus' toaster?"

"Yeah but it wasn't easy," said Steve. "Most of the people I know are either going to be at the wedding or for some reason had no desire to hang out all day with a grouchy alien robot."

"But you did get someone didn't you?" asked Jake.

"Yes. Actually he kind of jumped at the chance," said Steve. "I had to give him some money to entertain the robot with but at least he's doing it."

"Really? Who'd be crazy enough to actually want to do it?" asked Jake.

A knock sounded on the door of Varcus' ship and Varcus walked over and pressed a button and the door slid open. Outside stood a young man with long hair wearing a pair of ratty jeans, a sleeveless Metallica T-shirt and a red bandanna. He held up his hand, his thumb index and pinky fingers extended.

"Ola, alien dude!" said Johnny.

Chapter Twelve

Varcus and Larry entered the back of the little
Lutheran church, Varcus still wearing his blue suit from the
broadcast. Larry was dressed in a tight white leather uniform
trimmed in gold that made little crunching sounds as he
walked. The organist noticed the pair and hit a bad note and
stopped playing and before long a wave of whispers and head
turns occurred until everyone sat staring at them as the
church fell dead silent. Varcus and Larry looked around and
smiled at all the faces as Tommy the usher approached.

"Are you on the bride's side or the groom's?" asked
Tommy nervously.

Varcus looked confused, then leaned down and spoke
quietly to Tommy. "You mean humans even pick sides at a
wedding? No wonder you fight all the time," he said.

"Do you have special seating for celebrities?" asked
Larry hopefully.

"Uh, I just need to know if you're friends with the
bride or groom," said Tommy, who hadn't asked for any of
this.

"Oh. Well I have nothing against Cynthia but given
the fact she's made threats against my person perhaps we
should sit in the groom's section," said Varcus.

Tommy glanced around then walked Varcus and
Larry down the aisle as everyone stared. Varcus greeted
people with a nod of the head or hello while Larry strutted
and waved as if he was in a parade. When they got to the
fourth row from the front Tommy motioned for them to sit
and people slid down to make room, crunching together to

give the aliens a wide berth. Larry sat down then Varcus squeezed in, looking a little squished, as the organist resumed playing and the guests started talking again in quiet whispers.

Varcus looked around at the beautiful little church. Lavender and blue flowers and ribbons decorated the interior. Pastor Dave, a kindly looking grey-haired man in his late fifties, stood wearing his robes by the dais at the front of the room. People talked amongst themselves, some about the aliens but many about the wedding.

Varcus leaned over towards Larry. "You know there is quite the air of anticipation."

"I'm sure it helps they have two stylish and famous aliens in attendance," said Larry. "Well one anyway."

"Oh yes. As if wearing skin tight leather to the wedding was appropriate," snapped Varcus.

"At least I'm wearing wedding white and don't blend in with the decorations," argued Larry.

"I don't blend in," said Varcus huffily.

"You're right, you don't. You stick out like a handful of sore thumbs," said Larry.

"See here you little--" began Varcus rather loudly before several people in the vicinity shushed him. The two sat quietly for a moment then Varcus said "Look. Seeing as how we're stuck with one another I suggest we put aside our differences for the time being and try to get along."

"Agreed. Getting thrown out of the wedding would do little to bolster either of our reputations here on Earth," said Larry.

"Good," said Varcus. The two shook hands and sat back in the pew. "I'm quite looking forward to this. It should be an interesting experience. And I have to remember to thank Johnny for getting the robot out of my hair for a while."

"Who?" asked Larry, checking out a blonde in the third row.

"A nice young man that's entertaining my DA-42," explained Varcus. "He seemed very eager to help and that's rare these days. I think he'll be a very good influence on the robot."

"Explain this to me again," said the robot sitting on a bar stool in the Moosehead Tavern. "Why am I licking my hand?"

"Ya gotta wet it, dude," said Johnny. "Otherwise the salts gonna fall off."

"And why exactly do I want salt sticking to me?" asked the robot.

"So you can lick it off," said Johnny.

"I'm putting it on so I can lick it back off?" said the robot.

"Yeah, man," said Johnny.

The robot thought about this. "So basically I could put it anywhere I want as long as it sticks?"

"If that's your thing," said Johnny.

"Fine," said the robot. He leaned down and licked the bar then poured salt on it and sat back to look, satisfied with the results. "There."

Johnny shook his head and laughed. "You're one crazy dude, dude. We're gonna get along great."

The robot eyed Johnny suspiciously with his little black eyes. "We are?" he said.

"Yep," said Johnny, then he stuck out his tongue and gave the bar a good wet smear before pouring salt on it. He then picked up his shot glass with one hand and his lime wedge with the other. The robot watched him carefully and mimicked him. "To us! Two crazy dudes!" said Johnny.

The robot looked at Johnny and cocked his head to one side quizzically, then looked pleased at finding someone who actually seemed to like him for a change. Johnny licked the salt off the bar, drank down the tequila and bit into the lime before grimacing a bit. The robot watched and did the same but without the grimace.

"Hmm. Interesting," said the robot.

"What?" said Johnny.

"An intense burning sensation in my throat followed by an overwhelming impulse to gag," said the robot. "Then a weird but not altogether unpleasant feeling in my head."

"That's tequila alright. You want another?" asked Johnny.

"Tequila. Yes, I think I should try that again," agreed the robot. "For data."

Johnny looked down at the bartender and held up two fingers and pointed at the bar in front of him. "You mean the robot guy on Star Trek?"

"Who?" said the robot.

"Dude, you need to get out more," said Johnny.

The bartender poured the shots and served them along with two more lime wedges and Johnny and the robot licked the bar and poured salt on their respective puddles.

"To Data!" said Johnny, toasting the fictional android.

"To data!" said the robot, toasting non-fictional bits of information.

They licked the salt off the bar again, taking with it another herd of innocent germs that had been living there peacefully which were quickly annihilated by a wave of Cuervo.

Steve stood at the altar at the front of the church near Pastor Dave. The organist began to play *Canon in D* and all heads turned to watch as Mark came down the aisle accompanying Julia in her lavender bridesmaid's dress followed by Craig and Paula. Jake came next walking arm and arm with Nicole.

There was a pause and the music changed to *The Bridal Chorus*. Cynthia in white came slowly down the aisle accompanied by Pete. Jake glanced over at the aliens to see what they were up to. Varcus sat smiling ear to ear as Cynthia went past, obviously quite taken by the event transpiring around him. Larry appeared to be busy examining the bridesmaids.

Cynthia noticed neither of them as she walked by, too caught up in her day. When they got to the front she kissed Pete on the cheek and he sat down in the left front pew. Nicole came down and held Cynthia's train for her and she took her place next to a happy looking Steve in front of Pastor Dave as the organist stopped playing.

"Good afternoon," said Pastor Dave. "We are gathered to celebrate the marriage of Steve Anderson and Cynthia Larson. They have come here today because of the love they feel for one another and ask you to witness and share in their commitment to each other as they embark on their journey together. A journey of hope that looks ahead to their new future as one."

Varcus leaned over and spoke quietly to Larry. "This is so exciting!" said Varcus "Perhaps I should have brought the robot. He could have used some Earth culture to settle him down."

"Who knows? Maybe he's getting some Earth culture right now," said Larry.

The opening guitar riffs of *Sweet Child of Mine* rang out loudly through the bar as the robot jumped off his barstool and covered his ears.

"Aggh! What is that?" said the robot, wondering if this was some sort of auditory weapon the humans had secretly developed.

"A classic, man," said Johnny.

"Yes, but what is it?" asked the robot.

"Rock and roll, dude. Haven't you ever heard rock and roll before?" asked Johnny.

"Apparently not as I am still able to hear," said the robot.

"Dude! If we're gonna be buds you gotta learn to rock. This is Axel and Slash, man. G 'n R!" said Johnny.

"Okay. Just warn me next time that we are about to rock," said the robot. "My audio circuits almost overloaded. I've lowered my volume now."

"Well just so you have it up loud. It's got to be loud," said Johnny.

"It is loud. I can barely hear you," said the robot. He sat back down on his bar stool.

"Cool. Bartender! Dos margaritas por favor," said Johnny.

"What is a margarita?" said the robot.

"You'll like it. It has tequila," said Johnny.

"Good," said the robot.

Johnny leaned back on his bar stool and bit his lower lip and played air guitar, bobbing his head in rhythm to the music. The robot watched him and slowly began to do the same in mechanical fashion.

"Sweet, dude!" said Johnny. "Now you're rockin' Earth style!"

"Do you, Cynthia, take Steven Roger Anderson to be your lawfully wedded husband, to love and care for him, in sickness and in health, till death do you part?" said Pastor Dave.

"I do," said Cynthia.

Jake looked over at Nicole and she looked back at him and smiled.

"And do you, Steven, take Cynthia Patricia Larson to be your lawfully wedded wife, to love and care for her, in sickness and in health, till death do you part?" said Pastor Dave.

"I do," said Steve.

"The rings please," said Pastor Dave. Jake took a step forward and handed him the rings he was holding then stepped back. Pastor Dave held out both hands, one ring in each and Steve and Cynthia each took one then faced one another.

"Steven, with this ring I take you to be my loving husband," said Cynthia, placing the ring on Steve's finger.

Steve started to do the same, then dropped the ring but made a miraculous catch before it hit the ground as the church crowd chuckled. He recovered and slid the ring onto Cynthia's finger and said "Cynthia, with this ring I take you to be my loving wife."

"I present to you Steve and Cynthia Anderson, husband and wife," said Pastor Dave. "You may kiss the bride."

Steve laid a good long kiss on Cynthia as the people in the pews stood and applauded. The organist began to play *The Wedding March* and the wedding party made a two at a time exit out of the back of the church, Jake giving a small wave to the aliens as he went past.

Varcus took a silk handkerchief out of his pocket and dabbed at a tear in his eye. "That was quite moving. I guess I got carried away in the moment."

"My own manliness keeps me from such public displays" said Larry. "That's why I only watch *Rudy* in the privacy of my ship."

"Yes, that one gets me every time too," said Varcus. "What happens now I wonder?"

"If I know my weddings then now it's party time!" said Larry.

Chapter Thirteen

Varcus and Larry stood near the end of a long line going into the main room of the VFW. Varcus craned his neck out to look around the people to try and see what was going on up at the front. He pulled his head back in, then Larry did the same. Varcus did this once again then looked irritated and turned to Larry. "I thought you said it was party time," he said.

"It should be. Perhaps this is some form of line dancing I am not familiar with," said Larry. He tapped a teenage boy in front of him on the shoulder. "Excuse me, adolescent citizen. Could you tell me at what point this wedding business is going to become fun? We thought there were going to be festivities."

"There are. This is just the receiving line," said the boy.

"Ah," said Varcus. "So we're in line for our food and drink then?"

"No," said the boy snottily.

"What exactly is it we're doing here then besides showing off our queuing skills?" asked Larry. "I saw chicks. Where are they?"

"Look. It's hard to explain," said the boy. "The bride and groom and their parents are at the front of the line waiting to greet everyone."

Larry peered around the long line again. "Well can't they just wait until we're inside and greet us all at once?"

"That's not how it's done. We each talk to them personally," said the boy.

"I see. What are we supposed to say?" said Varcus.

"Most people say the same things. Congratulations. You must be very proud. It was a lovely wedding. That kind of thing," explained the boy.

"Seems like an awful lot of standing around just to say something everyone knows you're going to say anyway," said Larry grumpily.

"Then say something else," said the teen.

"Like what?" said Varcus.

"How should I know? Be original. You're the ones from another planet," said the boy.

"You know on Tweellar Two it is customary to serve the grooms' father as the main course at the celebration dinner," said Larry as he shook James' hand.

"That's...interesting," said James, looking a bit worried.

Larry nudged James in the ribs and winked. "Lucky for you you're on Earth, eh? At least for the moment," he said. He moved on to Carolyn. "And on Udal Major the groom's mother is ceremoniously dipped in Penoli oil then--"

Varcus quickly intervened and grabbed Larry by the arm and pulled him away. "Sorry. He's not from around here," he said.

"Yes, I'd guessed that," said Carolyn.

Varcus turned and found Cynthia next in line. "Ah, Cynthia," he said warmly. "We meet at least. I just wanted to say that--"

Cynthia interrupted him. "--and I just want to say that you better hope this wedding turns out to be like a fairy tale I'm going to remember for the rest of my life, no matter how short it turns out to be on this Gork place of yours or so help me you're going to be the sorriest alien who ever landed in my pasture. Understand, Mr. Martian?"

"Yes, ma'am," said Varcus quietly, edging away from Cynthia. He quickly shook Steve's hand then backed away.

"Would it help your wedding's fairy-taleness if I performed an alien abduction and stole the bride?" asked Larry. "I have a hot tub and champagne and an extensive Barry White collection and we could..." he said, trailing off under Cynthia's withering glare. "Maybe next time."

The alien duo moved off away from the line. "I think that went well," said Larry.

"Oh very nice," said Varcus. "I'm sure hinting at eating the groom's parents is a big hit at Earth weddings." He looked around the small crowded reception hall. "This way."

"Where are we going," said Larry.

"To the bar," said Varcus. "Come on, I need a drink."

"So this Farcon guy," said Johnny drunkenly to the robot. "He doesn't respect you much does he?"

"No he doesn't," slurred the robot back as he wobbled on his bar stool. "Always telling me what to do. Never asks me what I want to do. What my needs are."

"And you don't even have a name?" said Johnny.

"Nope. He just calls me robot," said the robot.

"Wow. Dude," said Johnny.

"Yeah, dude," agreed the robot.

"That'd be like my mom calling me human," said Johnny, taking a gulp from his margarita. He thought about it. "Although that would be better than most of the stuff she calls me."

"Duuude," said the robot, liking the word more and more. He took the umbrella out of his drink and stuck it behind his left ear, giving him a match to the one behind his right.

"You know what I'm going to do?" asked Johnny.

"Order more margaritas?" suggested the robot hopefully.

"No," said Johnny. "Well yes, but after that. I'm gonna give you a name."

"You are?" said the robot.

"I am. And then we'll have those cheeseburgers," said Johnny.

"So I can tell the Representative I am all that after all," said the robot.

"Right. Then we're going skateboarding," said Johnny.

The robot managed a dismount from his bar stool and stood up unsteadily. "Okay, but first I have to go to the can again." He giggled. "The can. I love that."

"Dude, you just went a couple of minutes ago!" said Johnny.

"I know. They must have outfitted me with a teensy-weensy synthetic bladder," said the robot.

"Maybe you can get an upgrade," said Johnny.

"Yeah I'll talk to Ficus about that too," said the robot. He took one step towards the bathroom and fell flat on his face with a loud clatter. "And maybe one for my feet," he said while pushing himself up off the dirty floor.

Johnny looked him up and down. "Hey, how do you..." he said. motioning his head towards the bathroom.

"Oh. Would you like to come in and watch?" asked the robot.

"Duuude! You never ask another dude into the bathroom with you. Only chicks do that," said Johnny.

The robot shrugged. "Okay," he said and staggered off towards the bathrooms.

"And go in the right one this time!" Johnny shouted after him. He turned back to the bar and picked up his margarita as the sound of girls screaming came from the direction of the bathrooms. "Too late."

Chapter Fourteen

The wedding had moved into the wind down phase, a smattering of guests still scattered around the ballroom. Jake, Nicole, Steve and Paula sat together at a large round table near the dance floor. They were watching Varcus who was up at the DJ and karaoke setup, microphone in hand, doing a passable version of *Old Time Rock and Roll* while Larry danced wildly about on the dance floor bouncing from one woman to the next.

"Don't you people do anything without Karaoke?" asked Jake.

"Not really, no," said Steve as Cynthia came back from her latest mingle and plopped down on his lap.

It had been an interesting wedding and Cynthia had mixed feelings about the whole affair. While Varcus hadn't consumed anyone and Larry had been on his best behavior, other than hitting on and dancing with just about every woman in the VFW, she was a little annoyed that all the attention hadn't been on her. This was after all supposed to be her big day and she had found it difficult to compete with Varcus doing the Hokey Pokey and Larry and his strangely compelling Rubber Chicken Dance.

"So this is the guy that's tossing us off the Earth," said Cynthia, who was having a hard time disliking Varcus in spite of her best efforts. For being an alien from another planet he had a down to Earth quality and had gotten along famously with everyone in attendance, especially the children who had followed him around like the Pied Piper.

"Weird huh? He's more like the crazy uncle that gets drunk and falls in the wedding cake," said Jake as Nicole snapped yet another picture of the aliens.

Paula ran her finger around the rim of her champagne glass. "I think he's kind of sexy. I wonder how he--"

"You're not sleeping with the alien," said Cynthia.

"Why not?" pouted Paula. "It is a wedding."

"Yeah it's a wedding, not a science experiment," said Cynthia.

"Well we are trying to find a way to get him to call the whole eviction thing off," Jake pointed out. "Maybe if she--"

"Forget it," said Cynthia.

"Party pooper," said Paula.

"He's sure been having a good time," said Steve.

"Yeah he sure has," said Jake. He turned to Nicole. "Do you think any of this is helping?"

"I don't know, but I guess it can't hurt," said Nicole.

"It can hurt my wallet. I'm almost out of cash from buying those two drinks," said Jake.

"But maybe if Varcus gets to know some humans he might be reluctant to move us," said Nicole.

"That's what I was hoping but we'll see," said Jake.

Cynthia got up off of Steve's lap again and held out her hand to him. "Come on, Stevie. It's time for you to go home and spend some quality time with your new bride."

"Yes, ma'am. That I can do," said Steve, taking Cynthia's hand and standing up.

"Don't do anything I wouldn't do," said Jake.

"You mean like get married? Too late," said Steve. He and Cynthia left arm in arm as Varcus wrapped up his song. He took a bow as Larry approached the stage.

"Go sit your vocal chords down before they do any more damage," said Larry. "Let an occasional viewer of *American Idol* show you how it's done."

Varcus looked annoyed but got off the stage and went over to Jake's table and sat down, his clothes a bit disheveled from hours of exuberant fun. He picked up a champagne glass and finished its contents and said "This karaoke is most enjoyable. I must say you humans really know how to throw a party."

"Some species don't?" asked Jake.

"Most species don't. They're all too busy being civilized," said Varcus.

"Guess us barbarians have something to offer after all," said Jake.

"No argument there," said Varcus.

The music started and Larry began to sing *I'm Too Sexy*, gyrating all over the small riser as the last of the female guests gathered under the stage and cheered him on.

"Now that's something I really didn't need to see," said Jake.

"Oh I don't know," said Paula sexily, and she stood up and sashayed towards the stage.

Varcus' PED beeped at him and he took it out and checked it, looking puzzled and concerned.

"Is something wrong?" asked Nicole.

"It's a message from the robot," said Varcus.

"What does it say?" said Jake.

"I'm not sure," said Varcus, staring blankly at the small screen. "It's long and rambling with a lot of exclamation points. It seems to be a series of references to shoving several of my appendages into a variety of my orifices."

"Can I see it?" said Jake.

Varcus gave the PED to Jake, who at that moment had the power in his hands to not only save the human race but to cure cancer, end hunger, get rid of both Osama Bin Laden and Jerry Springer and finally win the Cubs a World Series.

"Wow," said Jake, in reference to the message and not all his newly acquired abilities.

"Do you know what he's babbling about?" asked Varcus.

"Yeah, but I think you better talk to him about it," said Jake. "I try not to get involved in family disputes without a retainer." He handed the PED back to Varcus and the Cubs lost yet another opportunity.

"He may be malfunctioning. I better get back to the ship," said Varcus, standing up to leave.

"Wait, I'll come with you," said Jake, standing up as well. "You coming, Nicole?"

"You two go ahead," said Nicole. "I better stay and keep an eye on Paula."

Jake looked over at the stage which Paula had planted herself in front of, dancing sexily for a very interested Larry. "Good luck with that. You'll need it," he said, then headed towards the door with Varcus.

Chapter Fifteen

The robot hummed the chorus of *Highway To Hell* and leaned back unsteadily to admire his work. He was in a surprisingly good mood, surprising in that he had never been in a good mood before. He wished he had a mirror so he could look at himself again and see the blue bandana on his head, the holey jeans covering his spindly legs, the beat up Converse All Stars squeezed onto his feet and his already beloved Guns N' Roses Tee shirt. His new wardrobe had been a gift from Johnny who wasn't around right now, having left the robot alone to go searching for something called Twinkies.

The robot smiled a drunken smile as he thought about his new, only and first friend, then shook the paint can and started spraying the last "s" in "Varcus sucks" on the brick wall of the feed store. He finished it and was contemplating the aesthetic value of adding an exclamation point when red and blue flashing lights lit the wall and he turned and put his hands up in the air in surrender.

"Busted!" he said.

Chapter Sixteen

"Well he's not in there," said Varcus, immerging from the ship.

"I'm sure he'll turn up," said Jake, standing at the top of the ramp next to the ship's door. "Not many places he can hide, unless he gets a job as a crash test dummy."

Just then a sheriff's car pulled up into the driveway and over to the fence in the yard. Sheriff Johnson and Deputy Roberts got out and opened the back door and helped the robot out, still wearing his new old clothes, and supported him across the pasture over to the bottom of the ramp.

"I think this belongs to you," said Sheriff Johnson.

"I'm afraid so," confirmed Varcus.

"He! He belongs to you, not this belongs to you," protested the robot drunkenly. "Except I don't belong to him. I've just been letting let him boss me around because I haven't had anything better to do."

The sheriff and deputy let go of the robot go and he stood uncertainly for a moment before falling to the ground in a heap.

"I'm very sorry, officers," said Varcus apologetically.

"No worse than picking up my cousin Roy every Saturday night," said the sheriff.

Roy stuck his head out the back window of the sheriff's car. "Hey can we get going soon? It's almost time for me to puke."

"See what I mean? Good night," said Sheriff Johnson.

"Good night. And thank you, officers," said Varcus.

The sheriff and deputy walked over and got in the car and drove away, Roy waving out the window at the robot as they went. "Bye, little buddy! And don't forget to tell your boss I think he's a horses a--" said Roy, a couple of s's lost as the sheriff rolled up the back window.

Jake looked down the ramp at the robot lying face down in the grass. "Oops. Looks like someone had a good time."

"Robot! Pick yourself up and get up here!" demanded Varcus.

The robot tried to push himself up but couldn't muster it so instead slowly crawled up the ramp, metal hands scraping against its surface. When he finally got to the top Varcus stood glaring down at him, hands on his hips.

"Alright, robot, what do you have to say for yourself?" said Varcus.

"My name isn't robot," said the robot, totally inebriated. "It's Robb. Robb Ott."

"What on Kelgrin are you talking about?" asked Varcus.

"Dude. My name. It's Robb Ott (hic). Get used to it," said Robb.

"We'll see about that," said Varcus. "Turn off your simulation circuits immediately and get inside!"

"No," said Robb.

"No? What do you mean no?" said Varcus irritably.

"No as in no," said Robb. "I like being drunk and miserable. It feels good for some reason. I think I'm going to just wallow in it for a while."

"You sure that's a good idea?" asked Jake. "You know if you really do simulate humans..."

The robot made a gurgling sound and margaritas, cheeseburgers and Slim Jims suddenly tsunamied across the ramp towards Jake's shoes.

"That's what I was afraid of," said Jake, picking up his feet. "Man, that's just nasty."

"Sorry Jake," said Varcus.

"You got a mop in there?" asked Jake.

"Don't worry about it. After you leave I'll turn on the frictionless surface and it'll just slide right down the ramp," said Varcus. "You happy now, robot?"

The robot didn't answer and instead began mumbling random lines from *For Those About to Rock* as he put his hand up in the air, pinky, thumb and index finger extended.

"I guess that means yes," said Jake. "So, Varcus. Did you have a good time at the wedding tonight?"

"I certainly did, Jake. Very much so," said Varcus.

"And did you like all the people you met?" asked Jake.

"Oh, yes. They were all quite warm and kind, especially the children," said Varcus.

"So does this mean we can forget all about this whole silly eviction thing?" said Jake hopefully.

Varcus paused and looked at Jake. "No," he said. "But I did have a good time," he added brightly.

"Swell. Glad to hear it," said Jake.

"Don't let the man get you down, Jake (hic)," said the Robb.

"You be quiet," said Varcus.

"Monday morning we're going to get yanked out of here and brought to someplace that's going to make us all wish we could live together in Fargo instead and there's not a thing we can do about it," said Jake. "So yeah, the man's going to get me down."

"Damn the man!" said Robb, thrusting his fist into the air.

"Thanks for the moral support, Robb," said Jake.

"No problemo," said Robb. "You know, dude, you could always ask for a hearing."

"A what?" asked Jake.

"Robot..." warned Varcus.

"A hearing. It's your right as Representative. The man here probably didn't think it was worth mentioning," said Robb. "Damn the man!"

"Varcus? Is that true? Is there some sort of legal way I can fight the eviction?" asked Jake.

"Well, technically yes," said Varcus.

"Technically?" said Jake. "What does that mean?"

"It means that yes, you have the right to a hearing. But it's pointless. There's no way to fight the facts of GREEN's report, Jake," said Varcus.

"Well I want one anyway," said Jake.

"Why? It would just be a waste of time. And it would mean I'd have to postpone the eviction for another day," said Varcus.

"Boy, that would be a shame now wouldn't it?" said Jake.

"Yes it would," said Varcus.

"I like you, Varcus," said Jake. "I really do. But I like my planet better."

"If you liked your planet so much you'd let me do what's best for it and take you all off of it in a timely fashion," said Varcus.

"Then let me rephrase. I like *being on* my planet better. I want my hearing," said Jake.

"That's tellin' him, Jake (hic)!" said Robb. "Damn the man!"

"Thanks, but I think that's enough damning for now," said Jake. "So, Varcus?"

Varcus sighed. "Very well. As I said, it is your right. We'll leave tomorrow morning then."

"Leave?" asked Jake.

"Well we can't very well do it here now can we?" said Varcus.

"I don't know. I guess I don't know how all this works," said Jake. "Where are we going then?"

"To Kador, the galactic capital," said Varcus.

"As in another planet Kador?" asked Jake.

"Do you know of another one?" said Varcus.

"No, but I've got an atlas in my Humvee," said Jake. "I'd be glad to go check."

"You'll be going in front of the Galactic Council," said Varcus. "They'll decide if there's any reason not to evict you and your people."

"How much time will I have to prepare? I mean, if we're leaving tomorrow morning that doesn't give me much time to look for precedents, sleep, that sort of thing," said Jake.

"You can use the computer on my ship if you like. But the hearing will be tomorrow afternoon, unless we aren't able to get enough council members off the puttering lawns," said Varcus.

"Any chance for a postponement?" asked Jake.

"No," said Varcus.

"That's what I thought," said Jake. "Well can I bring someone with me? I could use some help on this. Steve and I used to be a pretty good team. He'd do all the work and I'd take all the credit."

"You can bring anyone you like, Jake, within reason," said Varcus.

"Good. I'll bring Steve then, if I can manage to get him on the ship. He's got a thing about flying so this space trip might be a toughie," said Jake.

Just then they heard the sound of a man and woman laughing and turned to look and found Larry with two of his arms strategically placed around Paula stumbling towards Larry's ship. The couple spied Jake and Varcus and Paula smiled a mischievous smile and waved as Larry gave a two handed thumbs up. The door to his ship opened and they disappeared inside.

"And on that note," said Jake, turning and heading down the ramp.

Varcus watched Jake until he went into the farmhouse, then stood quietly thinking about the broadcast he was going to have to give to the humans to explain the delay in their move before Robb's mumbled hummings at his feet interrupted his train of thought.

"And you! Robot!" said Varcus. "Get inside before the neighbors see you!"

Chapter Seventeen

Cynthia sat on the sofa next to Nicole in the living room surrounded by a healthy pile of wedding gifts. Steve sat on the floor nearby, already opened presents around him.

Cynthia ripped the wrapping off another box and examined at it. "Gee, a toaster. That'll be a big help on Gork," she said curtly and tossed it to Steve who added it to his pile. She quickly picked up another present. "Let's see what we have next," she said, tearing into the paper. "Oh look. A ceramic rooster. That'll be a big help on Gork," she said, throwing it at Steve.

"Glad to see you're taking things so well," said Jake who stood watching from a safe distance across the room.

Cynthia looked at Jake. "My parents and most of my friends went home to pack for the move so my gift opening party's a bust, there's a hung-over robot sleeping it off in the hammock in my backyard, and a few days from now I'll probably be running away from god knows what kind of alien creatures instead of going down water slides in my bikini getting a tan. So yeah, overall I think I'm taking it pretty well."

"Are you sure you don't want to come to Kador with us? I feel bad stealing Steve away the day after your wedding," said Jake.

"No I'll be fine here. Nicole and I can use a little girls with no aliens time. But if you run into Paula you could tell her I said to get her fanny home," said Cynthia.

"Yeah I wonder where they went," said Jake.

"Don't know," said Steve. "I went out early this morning to make sure the guys showed up to milk the cows and Larry's ship was gone."

"I thought you were watching her, Nicole," said Jake. "If you knew she was going to get down with an alien anyway the least you could have done was taken her and tossed her into Varcus' ship instead where she might have done us some good."

"It wasn't my fault. I turned my back for one second and they disappeared on me," said Nicole.

"I just hope they're here when we get back from this court thing. I don't have a clue what my argument is going to be and it'd be nice to have Larry's deal as a back-up plan if I can't fix this," said Jake.

"You'll just have to do your best," said Cynthia. "But in the meantime we'll be busy packing while you're gone."

"Thanks for the vote of confidence." said Jake. "Well I suppose we better get going," he said and picked up his bag.

Nicole stood up and walked over to Jake while Steve kissed Cynthia goodbye. "I know you're nervous about the case, Jake."

"Actually I'm not for some reason," said Jake.

"That's the spirit," said Nicole.

"No, I think that's the denial," said Jake. "Or Varcus' ray. Take your pick."

"You'll do fine. Here take this with you. For luck," said Nicole.

"Ah, your digital camera. How sweet," said Jake.

"My lucky digital camera," said Nicole.

"There's no hidden agenda here is there? You don't want me to take this with me so I'll bring you back a bunch of pictures of Kador do you?" said Jake.

"Nope. Just for luck," said Nicole.

"Right," said Jake. "Just be sure to mention me in your Pulitzer speech."

Nicole suddenly leaned over and gave Jake a peck on the cheek.

"Was that for luck too?" asked Jake, a bit surprised.

"No, the camera covered that," said Nicole.

"Then what was it for?" asked Jake.

"You figure it out," said Nicole, turning Jake around and pushing him towards the front door as he tried to do just that.

"I hope I don't get space sick and barf all over Varcus' ship," said Steve, picking up his suitcase and following.

"He's throwing us off the Earth. You have my permission to decorate his interior with bacon and eggs if you feel like it," said Jake. He opened the front door and walked out onto the porch and found Johnny skateboarding up and down the sidewalk.

"Dudes!" said Johnny excitedly. "Varcus is gonna give us a tour of the solar system!"

Chapter Eighteen

"That's Mercury," said Jake while gazing at the dusty looking brown and gold sphere rotating in front of him. He snapped yet another picture. "That's really the planet Mercury."

"You said the same thing when we came to Saturn, Jupiter, Venus, Mars..." said Steve.

"Yeah I know. But it's Mercury," said Jake still in awe of what he had seen today. The planets had all been incredible, although Pluto had been a bit dull which was why Varcus had zipped out to it first so they could work their way back in towards the good stuff. But while Saturn had been glorious and Jupiter had been spectacular, little planet Earth had been the most beautiful, a vibrant blue, green and brown sphere of life covered in swirling white clouds. Jake had a feeling that if everyone on Earth had a chance to go into space and see it from that perspective they might just park their cars, at least for a while, and go into the rainforest and give a tree frog a big hug.

"Hey, why don't you come over here? There's a much better view," Jake said to Steve who was sitting in one of the chairs Varcus had formed along the center wall. Varcus had taken the top down so everyone could get a better view and it had been disconcerting at first flying through space without outer walls, but Jake had gotten used to it and was now standing next to where the domed hull should have been visible.

"No thanks," said Steve, one hand tightly gripping the arm of his chair, the other tightly gripping his silver foil barf bag. "I can see everything quite well from here."

"Coward," said Jake.

"Dudes, I'm flying the ship!" said Johnny's voice over the loudspeaker system.

"On second thought maybe I'll join you," said Jake. Varcus had invited Johnny up into the cockpit after being blackmailed by Robb into bringing him along on the trip, something about hiding the keys to the ship.

"Hey, will this thing go upside down?" said Johnny over the speaker.

"Let's not find out, shall we?" Varcus replied. "Just follow the gauge and steer us out of the solar system."

The door to the other half of the ship opened and Robb came into the room and walked over to Jake. "I'm supposed to ask you if you would like some refreshments," he whispered.

"I don't know, what do you have?" asked Jake.

"Shush! Stop shouting!" said the robot.

"I'm not shouting," said Jake as quietly as he could. "Still feeling a bit under the weather are we?"

"More like I *am* the weather, something like a hurricane wrestling with a tornado," said Robb. "I have calculated that my head feels like it is four point six times larger than it actually is."

"Why don't you just turn off your simulation circuits?" said Steve.

"Johnny told me not to. He said if I'm going to be a righteous dude I have to learn to own the pain," said Robb.

"I don't know, I'd consider myself the most righteous dude on Earth if I could shut off my hangover the next day," said Jake. "Where did your clothes go by the way?"

"Varcus made me put them in the washer," said Robb sulkily. "Although I have to admit they were smelling a bit gamey after last night."

The door opened and Varcus walked into the room. "You're not honestly leaving Johnny alone to steer the ship are you?" asked Jake.

"Yeah, he's not exactly Mister Sulu you know," complained Steve who was getting paler by the moment.

"You wouldn't say that if you had seen him play *Asteroids* at the Seven-Eleven," said Robb.

"He'll be fine," said Varcus. "He can't really do any harm, space being such a big place and all that. That is unless he decides to do a u-turn and plunge us into the sun."

"I get the feeling he's liable to do that just for a thrill," said Jake.

"So how did you two enjoy the tour?" asked Varcus.

"Seeing the planets was nice but I could have done without some of the maneuvers, like when we whipped that u-turn around Titan," said Steve.

"That was Johnny's idea," said Varcus. "He wanted to see if we'd start going back in time. Something about beating someone named Tony Hawk to the punch and hordes of skater groupie chicks."

"The whole thing was amazing," said Jake. "Thank you, Varcus. You know it almost makes it worth being thrown off the Earth to see what we got to see today."

"You're most welcome," said Varcus. "I just came in to let you know I'll be displacing us into Kador's system momentarily and I should have us down on the ground in just a few moments."

"Thank God," said Steve, who planned to the minute they landed.

"If we were landing in a few minutes then why did you send me in here to see if they wanted something to eat? I'm going to go check on my clothes," said Robb, then he turned and trudged back out of the room.

"Did you just say we're landing in a few minutes? I haven't had a chance to prepare for my case yet," complained Jake. "I've been too busy being the first human to see, well, stuff."

"I'm sorry, but with this displacement drive interstellar travel times are almost nil," said Varcus.

"Well will I have some time after we land?" asked Jake.

"Yes, you should have an hour or so before the hearing starts," said Varcus.

"Perfect. One hour to come up with a defense to save the planet," said Jake.

"You mean the people don't you?" said Steve.

"I wish everyone would stop saying that!" said Jake.

"Hey, Varcus dude," said Johnny over the PA. "There's like this really, really big blip on the radar in front of us coming up really, really fast. What should I do?"

"Oops. Maybe I better get up there," said Varcus, heading towards the door.

"Yeah, maybe you should do that," said Jake.

"Please let me stand on the ground just one more time, please let me stand on the ground just one more time..." repeated Steve over and over into his barf bag.

Chapter Nineteen

Jake pushed through the turnstile and into the main area of Kador Prime Spaceport as Steve, Johnny, Varcus and Robb followed. He stopped and looked around, wondering when and if he was ever going to wake up. "This is crazy," he said. "I'm standing here on an alien planet a zillion miles away from Earth surrounded by hundreds of jet setting aliens and their luggage. Would somebody please explain to me how this happened?"

"You went off to pee," said Steve.

"Oh yeah. Remind me never to do that again," said Jake as a Fandorian family of fifty-five flippered by.

"There he is," they heard someone say and Bink Cruf, galactic wide famous reporter, pushed his way through the crowd and up next to Jake, closely followed by a multi-limbed camera alien.

"Who the hell are you?" asked Jake, suddenly feeling quite irritable.

"Bink Cruf here, bringing you another Mega News exclusive," said Bink, a weasel looking furry brown alien dressed in a silver trench coat and hat. "I'm here with Earth Representative Jake Williams who has just arrived on Kador for his monumental hearing before the Galactic Council. What do ya think, Jake, do you humans even stand a chance or are you just wasting everyone's time?" he said, shoving the microphone into Jake's face.

"Um-" said Jake.

"Dude, are we on TV?" asked Johnny, sticking his head momentarily into the picture until Varcus grabbed him by the shoulder and gently but firmly pulled him back.

"Would you like to comment on GREEN's damning report that human beings are no good self serving cannibalistic parasitical toxic beings that go out of their way to kill and torture anything green and/or living?" said Bink.

"What? That's not what the report said. At least I don't think it did," said Jake. "Anyway, humans are nothing like that. Well most of them anyway."

"So you don't terrorize and murder innocent dandelions?" asked Bink. "Or cut down well meaning fruit trees like that murdering s.o.b. leader of yours George Washington?"

"First of all, George didn't cut anything down and besides, he's long gone except for his picture on the dollar bill and the occasional furniture sale in his honor," said Jake. "And B, dandelions are far from innocent, believe you me. So third, get that microphone out of my face before I make you eat it."

"Then how would you respond to the story that's about to break that you yourself have sexually abused forty-seven percent of Earth's ring tailed lemur population and one blue whale who is now in undergoing extensive psychotherapy?" said Bink, ignoring Jake's threat.

"What?!" said Jake. "What idiot's going to report that?" he said, now feeling fully angry for the first time in days and quite enjoying the sensation.

"Yours truly, Bink Cruf, bringing you another Mega News exclusive" said Bink proudly.

"Then who told you?" asked Jake.

"I have my sources and they've asked to remain anonymous," said Bink. "But back to the Earth. Would you be willing to confirm that--".

Jake stewed for a moment then put out his hand and grabbed Bink around his rather skinny neck and pinned him against a nearby wall before he could finish. "How about you confirming who your source was for all this trash before *I* confirm that ringing your neck will actually shut you up once and for all," said Jake.

"Jake, calm down. Please don't kill the nice sleazy reporter," said Varcus.

"I'm guessing you don't have any kind of pacifying anything on me right now, Varcus, because I definitely and finally have some aggressive feelings going on," said Jake.

"No I don't. It would affect everyone around me here on Kador too so I can't use one," explained Varcus. "But I would consider it a personal favor to me if you would try and control your human urges and not assault everyone you meet."

"Sorry, can't help you there. Not till I'm done with this guy at least," said Jake.

"Well I tried," said Varcus, sighing. "I would suggest you tell him what he wants to know, Mr. Cruf. His species has a violence factor of nine point three on the Von Calix scale."

Bink gulped, which wasn't easy given the grip Jake had on his throat. "Alright," he squeaked. "It was my uncle Gurt."

"And where did he hear it?" asked Jake.

"How should I know? I don't ask my sources where they get their information. I just pay them for it," said Bink.

"Jake, you should probably know before you decide whether or not to strangle him that Bink's not the only vile and despicable reporter out there. Since everyone did away with their lawyers the media has gotten totally out of control," said Varcus. "They print or say whatever they want because there's no one left to sue them for liable."

"Well, it's not that different on Earth even with lawyers. Ask Angelina and Brad," said Jake. He let go of Bink and pushed him back into the crowd. "Wouldn't do any good to throttle you anyway then, another three of you would just pop up in your place. Just get out of here before I go totally Sean Penn on you."

"You'll be sorry you did that mister high and mighty Representative," said Bink. He turned to his camera squid. "Did you get all that?" he asked as they retreated out of sight.

Jake stood fuming and Steve walked up and put a comforting hand on his shoulder. "I'm sure no one believes what those guys report anyway, Jake."

"Oh no, people still believe it," said Varcus. "Because--"

"Because it's on TV," finished Jake.

"Yes," said Varcus.

"Hail, citizens!" said Larry, arriving on the scene. "Hey where did Bink go?" he asked looking around him. "I go to all the trouble of setting up this in depth and heart wrenching interview and he cuts it short?"

"You did that?!" asked and demanded Jake.

"Yes. No need to thank me," said Larry happily.

"Thank you? Why would I thank you?" said Jake.

"Because any publicity is good publicity," said Larry.

"Yeah I'm sure the court will be lenient now that they know I'm a lemur molester," said Jake.

"Eww," said Larry. "I'm no P.R. expert but I think you should have reconsidered before going public with your closet full of skeletal mammal abuses."

"I didn't go public with it!" said Jake.

"Then where did you hear it?" said Larry.

"On TV, where else?" said Jake sarcastically.

"Then it must be true," said Larry.

"We'll circle back to that one later," said Jake. "In the mean time, what have you done with Paula?"

"It would be ungentlemanly of me to recount in depth my latest conquest to you at this time. Perhaps over drinks later," said Larry.

"I don't want to know what you two have been doing," said Jake. "I just want to know where she is."

"Oh," said Larry, a bit disappointed in Jake's disinterest in his juicy details. "She's over at the shoe mall right now. She seemed very content to graze there with my Federation Fortune credit stick for an hour or eight."

"You gave a woman your credit card and told her to go shop? You're even stupider than I thought," said Jake.

"Are you saying that was a defective idea?" asked Larry.

"I don't know about space women, but yeah an Earth woman walking around alien shoe stores filled with new types of shoes she's never seen before holding your bank account

126

in her hand kind of spells financial wrath on a biblical scale," said Jake.

"Hmm. Perhaps I should be more vigilant and keep her company while she shops so I can check the pulse of my nest egg before it needs emergency resuscitation," said Larry and he scurried off back into the crowd.

Varcus looked at his watch. "Uh-oh, we're running really late now. That holding pattern we were stuck in ate up some of our time to begin with and the line at decontamination didn't help."

"Yeah that was a real treat. The guy could have at least warned me before he sprayed that crap all over me," said Jake.

"But necessary. You don't want to wipe out all us aliens with some stray Earth disease do you?" asked Varcus.

"Is that a trick question?" asked Jake. "So what are you telling me? I'm not going to have any time to prepare at all now?"

"I'm saying we have twenty minutes to get to you to court or they're going to declare a forfeit," said Varcus.

"And I'm guessing they won't be the ones giving up," said Jake. "Then come on, let's go grab a taxi. I'm dying to see what kind of illegal aliens you have driving your cabs."

Chapter Twenty

Jake, Steve and Varcus stood in the corridor leading into the main forum of the Galactic Council, Robb having escorted Johnny to the hotel where they would be staying that evening to avoid having either of them cause any problems.

"You'll have to wait in one of the antechambers, Steve," said Varcus, indicating one of the doors lining the hallway.

"You mean he can't even come in with me?" said Jake. "I thought he was coming along to help. All he's been able to do so far is divide his breakfast into little silver bags."

"Can I help it I forgot my Dramamine?" said Steve.

"Like that would have helped," said Jake. "You get motion sick on golf carts."

"I'm sorry, Jake. Only the Representative is allowed inside," said Varcus.

" I don't know if you've noticed but you say *I'm sorry* an awful lot," said Jake. "Either you're overly sensitive or you should rethink your lifestyle and try not to do so many things you need to feel sorry for in the first place."

"I don't think I'd be much help in there anyway," said Steve. "I've been racking my brain for some strategy for you to use but I've come up with a big fat lot of nothing."

"Same here, but if you would have come along the pictographs humans are going to scribble on the Gorkian cave walls before we all go extinct would have read *Jake and Steve blew it.* Now they're only going to mention me," said Jake.

"Sorry," said Steve.

"Don't you start too," said Jake.

"Anyway, good luck, buddy," said Steve. "Give 'em hell."

"I'd love to, but I think I'm going to end up being given it instead," said Jake.

Steve went into one of the waiting rooms and Jake and Varcus continued down the stone hall towards a large ornate archway. They walked through it and came out onto the floor of the forum of the Galactic Council. It reminded Jake of a Greek senate, a large round room with seats going upwards like a small basketball stadium, the ceiling an arched glass dome through which poured Kadorian sunlight.

"So this is a jury of my peers," said Jake, looking around the coliseum at the sea of two hundred or so wise looking white skinned white haired white robed androgynous beings that filled it.

"Pardon me?" said Varcus.

"An Earth expression. Being judged by a jury of your peers. And I'm not really sure this qualifies," explained Jake.

"These are still your peers," said Varcus. "We're all connected as sentient beings."

"If you say so. But I'm a little surprised. I thought this was some sort of inter-galactic council. They all look like they're from the same species to me," said Jake.

"Ah. I suppose that is confusing to you," said Varcus. "You see the beings you see here are not really here."

"I see," said Jake. "A lot like our government. When they bother to show up at all I think they spend most of their time having affairs with pages or roaming the halls looking for special interest groups who'd like to donate to their reelection fund."

"No, I mean they're not really here, here. They're not real," said Varcus. "They're holographic representations. You could call them avatars."

"Only if you'd like to tangle with James Cameron's legal team," said Jake.

"Then call them representatives of representatives," said Varcus. "You see that person over there for instance?"

"You mean the one that looks identical to the person sitting next to him who looks identical to the one next to him and the one next to him and the one next to him, etc, etc?" asked Jake. "Or are they all hers? I can't even tell."

"Yes, that's the one," said Varcus. "He could be anywhere right now. In his office on Plankin, at his summer place on Drevd, at his office on Baylon. And he could be anybody."

"I don't get it," said Jake. "Why would he be somebody besides who he is?"

"When a session such as this is called, a representative goes into a closed room wherever they are physically located," said Varcus. "The room will always have a chair, a holographic camera and a view screen so he, she or he-she can see the goings on here. The camera captures the persons words and movements and relays them and displays them as one of the figures you now see here in the council room."

"Is that so they don't have to actually be here?" asked Jake.

"Well, partially. Even though interstellar travel is now quite fast it is still fairly expensive," said Varcus. "But mostly it's done this way to provide anonymity for the council members."

"Anonymity? You mean you don't even know how your representatives vote?" asked Jake.

"For the most part no," said Varcus. "A computer even filters out any names, phrases or gestures they might let slip that might give away who they are."

"But that's ridiculous," said Jake. "They could be voting against everything they said they supported when they ran for office. Providing they even run for office out here that is."

"And how is that different from your own government?" said Varcus.

"Alright. You got me there. But at least on Earth we know they lied," said Jake. "I don't see how this is an improvement."

"Because here on the council everyone is able to vote for something because they think it's right, not because they feel obligated to because of their party or someone who helped put them in office. Oh everyone here has something they stand for and tend to support, but when a good idea comes along that belongs to someone else they don't vote against it simply because the other guys want it," said Varcus. He shrugged. "They don't even know which guys are the other guys."

"But isn't anyone worried that someone might get in here saying they stand for one thing then have it turn out they're a raving lunatic bent on some evil plot to dominate the galaxy and end up voting totally the opposite of what you thought they were going to?" said Jake.

"It has happened, but they never get very far," said Varcus. "Everyone that runs for office must first take a recorded oath of their stance on the issues. If they get elected a confidential record is kept of their votes which is constantly compared by a panel of judges to their platform oath, and if the two fail to match on a consistent basis they are immediately removed from the council."

"Interesting," said Jake. "I guess I can see the advantages. But it must be frustrating for your poor special interest groups. On Earth if you give a guy a couple million bucks you expect him to allow you to continue to dump chemicals into the Mississippi River. Here he might shut you down and you'd never even know he was the one who did it."

"Yes," said Varcus. "Too bad, eh?" A bell somewhere sounded three times and Varcus straightened his suit. "Well this is it, Jake. Are you ready?"

"No," said Jake, never being more sure of anything in his life.

"Good," said Varcus. "I'll be right beside you. I can't argue for you or act as a witness, but as Earth's sponsor I can answer informational questions regarding the case and any procedural questions you might have."

Jake took a deep nervous breath. "Okay. Let's get this over with," he said. He and Varcus walked into the center of the forum and stepped onto a slightly raised circular platform of red stone.

"Members of the council this is Jake Williams, Representative of the planet Earth," said Varcus, his voice somehow amplified. "He has come before you today as is his right to plead his case against the pending eviction proceedings against the humans of his world. Jake?"

Jake started to speak, then stopped, having no idea what to say and leaned over to Varcus. "What am I supposed to do?"

"Argue. Tell them why they shouldn't or can't move your people. That sort of thing," said Varcus.

"I know that. I just don't know where to begin," said Jake.

"I'm not really supposed to help," whispered Varcus. "But I would suggest just saying whatever comes to mind to start with. I think the rest will follow quite easily."

"Okay," said Jake. He thought for a short second, then said to the council members "Am I allowed to ask you a question?"

"A question?" asked one of them. "That would depend. Why don't you simply ask and we'll see."

"Alright," said Jake. "Here goes. Why are you moving us?"

"Why? I thought that was fairly obvious," said a council member.

"Not really. You see being from Earth I don't know anything about your laws, or even if this has to do with a law. All I know is there was the report from GREEN, a decision of some kind was made to move us and I was lucky enough to be the one served with the notice. But that doesn't tell me anything about whether or not it's legal," said Jake.

"I assure you it is," said a council member.

"No offense, but your assurances don't assure me much," said Jake. "I want to know exactly what you think gives you the right to do this."

"Very well," said a council member. "We have a statute in our laws, code one thousand seven hundred and sixty-four that not only gives us the right but impels us to do whatever we deem necessary to protect a life supporting planet, especially from its own inhabitants."

"Even if it puts those inhabitants in danger?" said Jake. "I get the feeling this Gork you're trying to move us to isn't going to be a barrel of laughs."

"No, it is in fact quite a harsh place," admitted a council member.

"That's what I was afraid of," said Jake. "So you put the well being of a sphere of rock ahead of living, breathing and thinking beings?"

"A life sustaining planet also lives and breathes," said a council member. "And it supports countless teeming numbers of living creatures that rely on it to sustain them. Unfortunately it can't defend itself past a certain point."

"But it can't think and feel like a human can," said Jake. "Sentient beings--"

"--are overrated," said a council member. "There have been a great many whom the galaxy would have been far better off without."

"But these are people and--" began Jake.

"Mr. Williams, the ethics of the law are not in question here. We are not sacrificing your people. You will have a new home and your race will survive if they work hard enough. We do value life," said a council member. "And if that is all you came here to say we'll be adjourning quite quickly."

Jake decided to try a new angle. "Well how about this. You know we human beings had no say in this statute of yours. Where I come from we all vote together on things and then live by the results."

"Really?" said a council member. "So I gather you're claiming the Indians, the Aborigines, and countless other races on Earth all sat down and voted to be pushed aside and/or massacred to make way for what was considered to be the needs of others?"

"You know about that do you?" said Jake, disappointedly.

"Yes, we know a great deal about the Earth and its history," said a council member. "Take human beings today. Even though your way of life has become an environmental threat to the planet and all life upon it including yourselves you continue to ignore it because it would be too inconvenient not too. You'd wipe yourselves out to do what you think is best for yourselves."

"But that should be our right," said Jake.

"Yes, you humans do go on and on about your rights don't you?" said a council member. "Unfortunately what you might consider to be your right is not always right."

"But you're throwing us off our planet!" said Jake passionately, a bit exasperated at not having any idea what else to say.

"Yes, and if humans found that hedgehogs could think and reason but were an imminent threat to your world you would show no hesitation in either moving them or wiping them out would you? That's all that we are doing," said a council member.

"But we've begun to make environmental progress now," argued Jake. "I admit it's come fairly slowly, but it's started. We just need more time."

"I'm sorry, but GREEN's report clearly states that having taken into account the calculations regarding the state of the environment, your so called progress and the social and governmental factors guiding your race that it is impossible for your people not only to fix things but to avoid doing irreparable damage to the planet in the future," said a council member. "There is nothing you can say to convince us otherwise."

Jake sighed and looked perturbed. "That's what this really all about isn't it?" he said. "That damned report. A bunch of numbers, graphs, pie charts--"

"There's no pie charts in the report," interjected Varcus helpfully.

"Thanks for clearing that up," said Jake. "You know what? You got me. You got all of us. We're human. We make mistakes, and sometimes they're whoppers. We tried to make life on Earth better for the majority of us and maybe we went about it all wrong. So go ahead and do what you're going to do because obviously I'm not going to be able to change your minds."

"Are you saying you're withdrawing your plea, Mr. Williams?" asked a council member.

"In a minute," said Jake. "First I want to tell you how impressed I was on the ride over here from the spaceport on the monorail. Your city is so beautiful, so clean. The air here is incredible. And Varcus tells me that you recycle ninety-seven percent of your waste?"

"That's correct," said a council member proudly.

"That's wonderful," said Jake. "Yours is definitely an ancient and wise culture."

"Thank you, Mr. Williams," said a council member.

"I've just got to ask you one last question if I may," said Jake.

"As you wish," said a council member.

"How long has GREEN been investigating planets?" asked Jake.

"A little over two hundred years," said a council member. "Why?"

"Two hundred years huh?" said Jake. "Not really that long in the scheme of things is it? I wonder how long it took to get Kador in the shape it's in today."

"What are you getting at?" said a council member.

"Just wondering what this planet and the planets you all come from were like when you *advanced species* were where we humans are in our technological age. Probably a good thing GREEN wasn't up and doing their thing back then, eh? Otherwise Gork would be a pretty crowded place by now wouldn't it?" said Jake. "You have a great and happy Kador day," he said before turning and walking angrily out of the council room.

Chapter Twenty-One

Jake stomped into Steve's antechamber and slammed the door behind him and stood there fuming.

Steve watched him calmly for a moment or two then said cheerfully "So how did it go?"

"Were you ever sent to the principal's office when you were a kid?" asked Jake.

"No," said Steve. "I didn't get into any trouble until I met you."

"Remind me to make you thank me for that later," said Jake. "But that's what it was like. You walk in and it doesn't matter what you say. She's the teacher, you're just a student and you shouldn't have crazy glued everything to her desk. The principal's mind is already made up, you're getting punished."

"So what you're trying to tell me is we're still getting punished?" said Steve.

"Yeah we're all going to be serving detention together on Gork," said Jake.

The door opened and Varcus came into the room.

"Don't even think about saying you're sorry," said Jake.

"I wasn't planning too," said Varcus. "You did what you could Jake. That was what I was trying to tell you last night, about the hearing being pointless. Your eviction is based on the findings of the report, and unless you could refute them somehow no one was going to change their minds. I'm sorry."

"Just couldn't help yourself could you?" said Jake. "It's not your fault though. Screwing up the environment was our doing and ruthlessly throwing us out of it is the council's doing."

"I'll take you to your hotel so you can rest, and in the morning we'll go back to Earth," said Varcus.

"Does our room have towels?" asked Jake.

"Of course. That's a bit of an odd question. Why do you ask?" said Varcus.

"Because we're going to swipe a few to take with us to Gork," said Jake. "We might as well get something out of this trip and I read somewhere they might be useful."

"Where did you read that?" asked Steve.

"Some book," said Jake.

Chapter Twenty-Two

Jake turned off the Multi-Sensory Uberdef Surround Pic TV after watching his interview with Bink for the sixth time. "That's about enough of that. Amazing how quickly you can get sick of yourself, especially from every conceivable angle."

"Try telling that to Terrell Owens," said Steve, taking a sip out of a bottle of something blue from the Translation Hotel mini-bar. "Or Howard Stern. Or a Kardashian or two. Or--"

"Yeah yeah, that's enough of the ego review I think," said Jake. "It does make me wonder though how much of Gork Trump has already bought up by now."

"I'm sure he's got architects working around the clock on the design for Trump Cave," said Steve, standing up. "I'm going to go see if I can find an ice machine around here. This Workleberry juice isn't half bad, but it's awfully warm. You need anything Jake?"

"Do you really have time to wait while I answer that question?" said Jake.

"Never mind," said Steve. "Johnny, how about you? Johnny? Yo, Johnny..." he repeated at Johnny who was sitting over in a corner playing with a hand held device of some sort.

"No, I'm good," said Johnny finally.

"I'll be right back," said Steve. He walked over to the door and pressed the open button but the door didn't seem to care. He pushed it again, and again, and again but the door continued to ignore him. "Okay, I guess I won't be right back. I seem to be having problems with leaving so maybe I shouldn't push myself too hard."

"What's wrong?" asked Jake.

"I think the door's broken," said Steve.

Jake got up and walked over to investigate. He pushed the open button, then did it again, and again, and again as if repeating the same action over and over was going to help. "I think you're right, although I thought doors were one of those things that couldn't *be* broken."

"Progress I guess," said Steve.

"Is the light green or red?" asked Johnny without looking up from whatever it was he was doing.

Steve examined the panel on the wall. "Red," he said.

"That means it's locked," said Johnny.

"Well how do you unlock it?" asked Jake.

"If it's locked from the inside you push the open button," said Johnny.

"We have been but it's not listening. How do we get its attention?" said Steve.

"Then it's probably locked from the outside again," said Johnny.

"What?!" said Steve. "You mean we're locked in here?"

"Yep," said Johnny calmly.

"How the hell did that happen?" asked Jake.

"Varcus did it to keep us from wandering around," said Johnny.

"Why that little purple..." said Jake. "Now I'm angry. I could've maybe lived with them throwing us off the Earth but now they're locking us inside cheesy hotel rooms."

"Yeah, I feel kind of insulted. I don't know about you but I wasn't even planning on wandering around," said Steve.

"I wasn't either, but now I want to wander all over the place," said Jake. "Maybe we could break a window."

"Yeah, and then what? Shimmy down the side of the building one hundred and eighty-seven stories? No thank you. I get dizzy just looking out the window," said Steve.

"There's a surprise," said Jake.

"Dudes. Chill," said Johnny.

"I don't feel like chilling," said Jake. "In fact I feel like being the total opposite of chilled, now that there's finally nothing forcing me to be it. I'm sure you'd be content to just sit there and play video games all day but I want out of here now that I can't get out of here."

"I'm not playing video games," said Johnny.

"Then what's that you're messing with?" said Steve. "Why don't you try doing something useful for a change."

Just then the door they had been arguing with slid open and Robb stepped into the room. "Well, are you coming or not?" he said.

"Dude," said Johnny to Steve. "You were saying?"

"So you can talk to Robb on that thing, Johnny?" asked Jake as they exited the hotel lobby doors and entered Two Hundred and Forty-Seven D Street.

"Yeah Robb gave it to me in case I needed anything," said Johnny. "It came with him when he was purchased so Varcus could get a hold of him but he just uses his PED instead."

"You two are getting to be good friends aren't you?" said Steve.

"He's my bro," said Robb, dressed again in his new old clothes.

"Yeah he's pretty cool for a machine," said Johnny.

"Probably because he wasn't programmed by Bill Gates," said Jake. "Although I wondered there for a while."

"Johnny taught me to chill out," said Robb.

"That's what I need to do," said Johnny.

"You? What's wrong with you?" asked Steve.

"They confiscated my board at the spaceport," said Johnny, like totally bummed out. "That customs lizard dude said it was illegal contraband."

"Are they going to give it back to you when we leave the planet?" asked Jake.

"Yeah, but I don't have it with me now. We've never been apart for so long," said Johnny.

"Gee, that's too bad," said Steve, managing to come close to approaching being able to sound sincere. "So now what?" he asked, wondering what to do now that they were standing on an alien street instead of being locked in an alien hotel room.

"That's a good question," said Jake. "My plan only went as far as getting to the other side of our hotel room door. I've been winging it ever since." He looked around at the capital city of Kador Prime. It wasn't really all that different from Chicago he thought, other than the fact that it was clean, had no cars driving on its streets and had beings milling about from every corner of the galaxy instead of every corner of the world. And the buildings were still tall and glassy, they just reached up into the sky another hundred stories or so and blotted out even more sky. He took out the camera and snapped a quick picture of the city for Nicole then put it away again. "I don't know about anybody else but I could use a beer."

"Yeah, after all we are only on an alien planet with a thousand new wonders to see. Might as well go sit in a bar and get drunk instead," said Steve.

"That's what I was thinking. Besides, maybe they'll have a thousand new alcoholic wonders to drink," said Jake. "Robb, any idea where there might be a good place around here? And please don't tell me this is a dry planet or I'm definitely going to lose it."

Robb shrugged. "How should I know? I just had *my* first drink yesterday."

"I know, but can't you interface with some central computerized Yellow Page directory or something?" Asked Jake.

"Who do I look like, R2-D2?" said Robb.

"How do you know about him?" asked Steve.

"I inputted all of Johnny's DVDs into my memory banks" said Robb.

"I suppose I can just ask someone," said Jake. He looked over the crowd going by and tried to find something that didn't look like it would just as soon excrete alien mucus all over him as to talk to him. "Excuse me, err sir," he said hoping to at least get that part right. "Can you tell me if there's a good bar around here?"

The being stopped and turned and four eyes glared at Jake. "Sir?! Hmpf. Some nerve. Just ignore me why don't you?" said one of its two heads in a decidedly female voice.

"Yes, that's my wife you're not talking to," said the other head in a masculine tone. "If I had time I'd teach you some manners."

"I'm sorry. I didn't see your other head," said Jake.

The alien harrumphed and twirled around and stomped haughtily off.

"What the hell was that all about?" asked Jake.

"That was a Pairadian husband and wife," said Larry. "They share a body at marriage."

"I bet that's a messy divorce," said Jake. "Hey wait a minute, where did you come from?"

"The spaceport," said Larry.

"Still? What did you get lost? I thought you were going to go shopping with Paula," said Jake.

"I did, but she became agitated when I asked a Nerokian sales girl for her number," said Larry sulkily. "And then after I told a Gradoll chick she had nice figures she made me take her home."

"You hit on two other women while you were with Paula?" said Steve.

"No four," said Larry. "Would you like to hear about the other two too?"

"Thanks, maybe later," said Steve.

"So is she at your place then?" asked Jake.

"I don't have a place here. They revoked my alien citizenship years ago," said Larry. "I took Paula home home, back to Earth. That's why I was coming from the spaceport." He sniffed. "I miss her already!"

"How did you know where to find us?" asked Steve.

"Where else would you be?" asked Larry.

"Never mind that," said Jake, now wanting a drink more than ever. "We still need to find a bar. Any suggestions, Larry?"

"Rokko's. Two blocks that way, one block left," said Larry. He checked one of his watches. "Happy hour starts in six minutes."

"Alright everyone, this way. Stay together and don't look the aliens in the eye, no matter how many they have," said Jake, heading down the street. "Your Representative's only head needs numbing."

Chapter Twenty-Three

Jake and his posse plunked down around a large round table in Rokko's Lounge. Jake picked up a table tent and looked it over, unable to recognize anything on it. "So what's good here, Larry?" he asked.

"I don't know, I've never been to this place," said Larry.

Jake stared at him. "Then why did you suggest we come here?"

"Because there was a sign across the street from where we were standing when you asked that said *Come to Rokko's Lounge, best happy hour in town starting at six o'clock, ladies night every Tuesday*," said Larry.

Robb suddenly made an odd beeping sound.

"Excuse you," said Jake. "You need a Tums or something?"

"No, I'm fine. Fartus is paging me though," said Robb. He sat with his head cocked to one side as if listening. "He's at the hotel. He wants to know where the photon everyone went. Should I tell him to go engage himself in some lewd bodily function?"

"Thanks, but you can go ahead and tell him where we are," said Jake. "We're not hiding, we're just not sitting back in that room just because he wants us too."

"Okay," said Robb, sending off a message back to Varcus.

"Hello, boys," said a tall willowy green waitress with long flowing golden hair, sparkling emerald eyes, and big round ears like a teddy bear. "My name is Cleeva and I'll be your waitress. Would you like to hear our--". She stopped in mid-sentence as she noticed Jake and her eyes grew wide in recognition. "You're the human from Earth! The one who--"

"I don't molest lemurs!" protested Jake.

"I can vouch for that," said Steve.

"Oh," said Cleeva. "And that other creature?"

"Wouldn't even know where to begin with a whale," said Jake.

"That I can't verify. He might've looked it up online," said Steve.

Cleeva tsked and looked irritated. "Isn't that just like the news today?" she said disapprovingly. "Always just making things up for ratings. So what can I get for you gentlemen?"

"Tequila!" said Robb enthusiastically.

"What?" Cleeva asked.

"Tequila?" said Robb hopefully.

"I don't think we have that," said Cleeva.

"Bummer," said Robb depressingly, finishing his sprint through the emotions for the moment.

"Do you have anything that resembles beer?" asked Jake.

Cleeva thought for a moment. "How about a couple of beakers of Fleb?"

Jake looked at Larry who he thought despite all previous indications to the contrary was most likely to be of help here.

"Fleb. It's cold and fizzy and people drink it while watching sports," said Larry.

148

"Sounds like a winner. A couple of pitchers of Fleb then," said Jake.

"Beakers," said Larry.

"Whatever," said Jake.

"What kind of Fleb do you want?' asked Cleeva.

"You mean do I want the king of Flebs, a light Fleb that tastes great and is less filling, or a Fleb that actually has some taste and wouldn't make an Irishman gag?" asked Jake.

"No I mean do you want Fleb One, Two or Three?" asked Cleeva.

"What's the difference?" asked Steve.

"Well if you're going to be operating power tools later you'll want to stick with Fleb One. If you're out for a good time, good conversation and a warm fuzzy glow with semi-decent hand-eye coordination I would suggest Fleb Two," explained Cleeva. "But if you just lost your girl, your job--"

"Your skateboard," said Johnny.

"Your planet," said Steve.

"--then you probably want to say the heck with my higher brain functions and the ability to walk just give me some Fleb Three," said Cleeva.

"You sold me," said Jake. "Bring on Fleb Tres porfavor senorita."

"Coming right up," said Cleeva, turning and heading towards the bar.

"Hey how did she know what I just said?" said Jake. "I was speaking Spanish."

"But she probably heard Poota, her own language unless she happens to speak something else," said Larry.

"There are translator satellites orbiting this and every other planet in SOW."

"SOW?" asked Steve.

"Yes, one of those pig things you'll be representing in court in Annandale," said Jake.

"Would've been representing in court you mean," said Steve.

"SOW stands for Society of Worlds," said Larry.

"Catchy," said Jake. "So it didn't matter what I spoke, English, Spanish, Pig-Latin or Swahili it was going to come out as Poota to her?"

"Yes," said Larry. "Varcus and I use personal versions when we travel."

"We could use one of those over the Earth so we could understand what the hell all those telemarketers are trying to sell us," said Jake.

"Hey how are we going to pay for all this?" asked Steve, realizing the translator probably wasn't going to be able to do much for the greenbacks they were carrying.

"Crap! I suppose my platinum card isn't going to impress them much here is it?" said Jake.

"Maybe I can help," said Larry. "Jake, have you decided about my generous offer to gallantly save everyone on your planet yet?"

"No, and I really don't want to talk about it right now other than to say that it's looking a helluva lot better at this point," said Jake.

"Glad to hear it. But we just did. Talk about it that is. Now I can write the evening off on my taxes as a business expense, so don't worry everything's on me," said Larry.

"You still pay taxes out here? I thought you were all so advanced," said Steve

"No one's that advanced," said Larry.

Jake surveyed the room to gather important drinking information such as where the bathrooms were in case Fleb used the same fast track through the body as beer. He made a mental note they were next to the table in the far corner and was about to rejoin his own table's conversation when he noticed that the three spiked aliens sitting there in business attire were all talking but apparently not to one another. He wondered stupidly at first if it wasn't some form of telepathy then decided it wasn't important anyway until he glanced around and found that many of the other beings in the bar were doing the same thing. "Hey, Larry. Why are so many people in here talking to themselves? Are they sharing a brain or something?"

"Some of them might be. But most of them are just talking on their self fones," said Larry.

"Self phone? Oh you mean like a cell phone," said Jake. "I suppose I can't see them because they're so small and hiding in their ears."

"No, you can't see them because they're so small and hiding in their heads," said Larry. "Many people choose to have self fones installed in their children at birth."

"That's terrible!" said Steve.

"Best way to stay connected," said Larry.

"Do you have one?" asked Jake.

"I did, but I had it removed because it wasn't working. My manly chin was blocking reception," said Larry. "Now I have to use my PED. Who knows what important details I might be missing about my friends lives such as what they are having for dinner or what cute thing their kidling just did to the family catoid."

Cleeva came back with glasses and two big beakers of a gold colored bubbly liquid and put them on the table. "If you want me to start you a tab I'll need someone's credit stick in case you all pass out," she said and Larry handed his to her and she moved on to another table.

"Thank the spirits I got that away from Paula when I did," said Larry. "You were right, Jake. She was glad to see me because she was having trouble carrying everything and with my four muscular arms she said she was finally going to be able to do some real power shopping."

"I told you so," said Jake.

Larry sniffled again. "But I still miss her," he said sadly. "She did this thing with her hair where she twirled it around her finger and this thing with her tongue where she twirled it around--"

"Ahhh! Stop right there. That's too much information," said Jake, grabbing a beaker then filling up glasses and passing them around.

"--her spoon when she ate Bolarian Mint freeze," finished Larry ignoring Jake's request for conversation brakes. "That was too much information?"

"From you, yes," said Jake. "But then most anything is."

"And if you like her so much then stop hitting on other women all the time!" snapped Steve irritably.

"What's gotten into you all of a sudden?" asked Jake.

"I miss Cynthia," said Steve. "It's the day after my wedding and she's light years away and this bonehead keeps complaining that the gorgeous woman he's infatuated with is mad at him because he can't stick to just her."

"It would be selfish of me to keep myself to myself," protested Larry. "And I'm not a bonehead."

"Yes you are," said Jake, holding up his glass and examining it. "Well, it looks more or less like beer," he said, then took a tentative taste. "Hmm."

"Well?" said Steve, not about to touch his own Fleb until someone else tried it and refrained from spitting it across the table or having their head explode.

"Ok, so it's not beer after all," said Jake.

"It's not tequila either," said Robb sulkily after sampling his.

Jake tried it again. "Actually it tastes like Coke."

"Coke Coke or coke coke?" said Steve suspiciously. "As in am I supposed to drink it or sniff it?"

"Or lick it off the bar," said Robb.

Jake looked at Robb but decided he didn't want to know. "I just tastes kind of like cola. Try it."

Steve picked up his glass and gave it a sip. "You're right it does."

"I guess the big brewers out here in *Futurama* finally got beer to taste exactly instead of almost like pop," said Jake.

"Actually Float Cola and Beeb Beer merged after the great beer and cola wars of the thirties," said Larry. "They were the giants left standing in their respective industries and when they finally made peace they combined their products into one."

"So you used to have beer out here in la la land?" asked Jake.

"Yes. Sadly it's gone. Earth is one of the last backwater places you can still find it,' said Larry.

"For the next two days or so," said Steve.

Just then Varcus stormed into the bar and up to the table. "There you are! I'm very angry with all of you. Especially you robot for letting them out."

"So what else is new?" said Robb in his recently learned who gives a flying whatever voice.

"Get up. You're all going straight back to the hotel," said Varcus.

"But I don't have a room there," said Larry.

"Not you, you idiot!" said Varcus. "Everyone but Larry. Come on. Now. Up. Let's go."

The table ignored him and sat drinking their Flebs.

"Stand up. Time to go. Gotta get a move on. Can't have you Earthlings all exposed to oh the hell with it," said Varcus and he pulled a chair over from a nearby table and sat down with his not to be moved charges.

"Cleeva! Another glass over here," said Jake.

"So. I suppose it's happy hour isn't it?" asked Varcus. He looked around the table and found a lot of somber faces. "Maybe not. What's wrong?"

"Let's see," said Jake. "Larry misses Paula, Steve misses Cynthia, Johnny misses Rosebud, Fleb isn't tequila and I screwed the pooch in court today and am going to go down in history as the person who lost the Earth once and for all. Does that about cover it?"

"I think I'm developing a rash too," said Larry.

"Again with the too much information from you," said Jake. "But anyway, we're all going to get drunk. Good and drunk."

"Fleb Three?" asked Varcus, looking at Jake's glass.

"You got it," said Jake.

"Well I just got chewed out by the council for bringing you here so I'm not having the best of days either," said Varcus.

"I thought it was our right to have a hearing," said Steve.

"It is, but you aren't supposed to know about it and just because someone's robot blabbed about it doesn't mean the council is very happy with me you found out," said Varcus.

"Live with it, dude," said Robb.

"And his name is Robb," said Johnny.

Varcus sighed. "Fine. I'm tired of arguing about it. From now on I promise to call you Robb."

"Then we're cool," said Robb.

"Good," said Varcus.

"For the moment," said Robb.

Varcus shook his head. "You know I remember when my life used to make some kind of sense," he said as Cleeva dropped off another glass at the table.

"Welcome to the club," said Jake, pouring Varcus a Fleb and sliding it towards him.

"I really shouldn't," said Varcus.

"Drink," said Jake, taking a drink of his own.

"This is Fleb Three and I have to fly tomorrow," said Varcus.

"Drink," said Steve.

"And what if someone with authority comes in here and sees me drinking with a bunch of Earthlings who aren't even supposed to be on the planet let alone in one of its bars," said Varcus.

"Wuss," said Robb.

Varcus glared at him. "Fine. I'm just having one though," he said. "There is no way I'm getting totally wonkered tonight."

Chapter Twenty-Four

"You're wrong! You're absholutely wrong!" slurred Varcus. "The shecond Alien movie was directed by James Cameron, not Ridley Shcott," he said.

"Are you shure?" said Larry, equally inebriated.

"Absholutely," said Varcus.

"How do you two aliens know so much about Earth movies?' asked Jake, quite happy in the head himself but able to still speak relatively clearly after years of intensive training.

"HBO, Cinemax, Turner Clashic," said Varcus. "They're all eashy to pick up in space off the Earth communications shyshtem."

"Don't forget the Playboy channel," said Larry.

Varcus reached out and managed to grab the beaker from the center of the table on only his second attempt and tried to pour himself his ninth Fleb of the evening but only a couple of drops dribbled out. "Dang it! Out again."

"More Fleb!" shouted Larry, who was turning out to be exactly the kind of drunk that Jake had feared he would be.

Steve started snoring again and Jake lightly whacked him on the back of his head. "Wake up."

"But I'm tired!" complained Steve, opening his eyes and yawning.

"All this started the last time you passed out on me so you can just push through tonight," said Jake. "What we need is some music to liven things up."

"There is music," said Johnny.

Jake listened. "You call that music? It sounds like Britney Spears and Eminem mated. And this is about the fifth time I've heard this same song. You could try playing something different next time on the jukebox."

"Dude, I did," said Johnny, who had switched from Fleb to Neutron Energy drink and was now as wired as he had ever been in his life. "I didn't know what to play so I just picked six different songs by six different people."

"More Fleb!" shouted Larry, drawing a few more glares from various aliens around the bar.

"Well they all sounded the same to me," said Jake.

"They are the shame," said Varcus. "More or less. The mushic industry started playing it safer and shafer, putting out mushic that fit a proven formula. They're down to one song now that they jusht change a little bit each time shomeone puts it out."

"Always wondered and worried what the future of Earth music was going to be like," said Jake. "Now I know. Probably a good thing we're being put out of our misery before we get any further down that road ourselves."

Cleeva brought two more beakers of Fleb over and put them on the table.

"Thank you," said Jake, wise enough to always treat his bartenders and waitresses with loving care.

"You're very welcome," said Cleeva, a bit of flirt in her voice.

"More Fleb!" shouted Larry.

"Dude! Look in front of you," said Johnny, who also was beginning to get irritated with Larry in spite of his uber laid back persona.

"I know, it's more Fleb!" said Larry happily. "That's what I said."

Steve watched Cleeva walk away then turned and looked at Jake. "She's pretty isn't she? In a greenish sort of way."

"Who, Cleeva? Yeah I guess she is," said Jake.

"I didn't know about the ears at first but they grow on you," said Steve. "They're kinda cute."

"I suppose so," said Jake.

"I think she likes you," said Steve.

"Maybe," said Jake.

"Are you going to go for it?" said Steve.

Jake looked at him. "Aren't you the one who's always telling me I'm going to get in trouble if I keep messing around with so many women? And now you want to know if I'm going to pick up some alien chick in a bar?"

"Well? Are you?" asked Larry.

"No," said Jake. "I wasn't planning on it."

"Good. I didn't want to break your heart when I shtole her out from under your nasal orifice," said Larry, taking a drink of Fleb but missing his mouth and pouring most of it down his chin and blue silk shirt.

"Yeah, you're just reeking sex appeal right now," said Jake.

"Thanksh," said Larry, stuffing a whopping handful of some greasy sauce covered Spam like meat balls into his mouth.

"Oh I get it," said Steve.

"Get what?" asked Jake.

"I get why you're not interested in a hot green alien chick with cute ears," said Steve.

"I suppose you're going to tell me, aren't you?" said Jake.

"You've got a thing for Nicole, don't you?" said Steve.

"No I don't!" protested Jake.

"Sure you do. I've seen the way you two look at each other," said Steve.

"Why how does she look at me?" asked Jake.

"See? You love her don't you," said Steve.

"Now you're being stupid," said Jake.

"Jake and Nicole, sitting in a tree, k-i-s-s-i-n-g," sang Steve.

"First of all, there aren't going to be any trees to sit in pretty soon," said Jake. "At least not friendly Earth type ones. And second, shut-up or I'm telling Cynthia about your Jessica Alba dreams when we get back." Steve immediately stopped sing-songing and Jake was left with the jukebox which he found was almost worse. "And third, can't we do anything about the music? If I have to hear *You're my hot thing and you make me sing when our love takes wing and we do our thing* one more time I'm going to end all of my problems but one and commit hari-kari."

"Dude, do you have your Ipod with you?" Robb asked from his face plant position against the table top, the Fleb in his bio system having done almost as thorough a job as tequila.

"Of course dude, always," said Johnny.

160

Robb pushed himself into an upright position with some difficulty and opened a small panel in his chest and pulled out a wire and handed the end of it to Johnny. "Plug it into this."

"Will it fit?" asked Johnny.

"Of course. Three point five millimeter mini-plug, universal standard." said Robb.

Johnny plugged in his IPod and the screen lit up. "Cool!" said Johnny, looking through the menu.

"In an emergency my head can be used as a six hundred watt boom box," said Robb.

"Play something good," said Steve.

"Yeah, yeah, I'll play something you old guys can enjoy too," said Johnny, and seconds later Robb/Bob Marley began singing about one love and three little birds.

"Ahhh," said Jake, closing his eyes. "You're my hero, Robb. Now maybe I can relax."

"More Fleb!" shouted Larry.

"Or not," said Jake.

"Hey, you!" said a gruff grumpy sounding voice.

Jake leaned back and listened to the music, hoping whoever it was was addressing someone else at the table other than him.

"Hey, human!" said the voice again, narrowing it down to one of three people.

Jake imagined birds and beaches and Nicole in a bikini.

"Hey, Representative!" said the voice.

"Crap," said Jake. He opened his eyes and found four to eight large blue and yellow spotted aliens, depending

161

on how many heads would end up belonging to how many bodies, standing behind him looking angry. "Yeah?"

"You are the Representative of Earth, right?" said the alpha male in the alien group. "That planet Bink was talking about on TV that's full of eco terrorists? You know me and the boys here don't like eco terrorists."

"Is that a fact?" said Jake, closing his eyes again and suddenly feeling like he was in a seedy bar on Tatooine.

"Yeah it is. And we don't like him either," said another of gang.

"You'll have to be more specific than that," said Jake calmly, wondering what Bob Marley would do right about now.

"The one with the big mouth," said the alien.

"Oh you mean Larry. We don't like him much either," said Jake.

"Hey!" complained Larry.

"And we don't like robot trash much either. Especially in our bar," said the alpha alien.

Jake opened first one eye, then the other, then stood up.

"Jake, please shit back down and try to ignore them," said Varcus. "They're Bufirts. Their race's favorite pass time is going around picking fights with other shpecies."

"It's okay. I got this," said Jake. "You know the metal dude's name you're talking about is Robb."

"He's a garbage disposal with feet," said the second alien.

Robb stood up quickly and wobbled angrily at the aliens. "You take that back or--" he said before falling over.

"Make me, circuit head," said the alien.

"Dude, I think now might be a good time to turn off your simulation circuits," said Johnny under his breath.

"But you said--" began Robb from the floor.

"Just do it," said Johnny, eyeing the gang who looked even more unfriendly than before.

Robb made a mental maneuver and his head instantly cleared. He stood up and put Johnny's IPod inside his chest compartment and closed it for safe keeping.

"Look guys. Let's all be real civilized here, shall we?" said Jake. "We don't want any trouble. Why don't you go sit back down and Larry'll buy you all a drink. Just listen to the music. Like Bob's saying we can all get along if we try."

"Yeah? I don't think so," said the alien.

Jake sighed. "Come on. Why not?"

"Because your music sucks too," said the alien.

Jake stared at him for a moment, then leaned in close to him and spoke slowly and quietly. "Be real careful now. You've insulted me, my species, one of my friends and one of those guys you just kind of end up hanging around with no matter what you seem do. I could maybe live with all that. But that's Bob Marley singing. So choose your next words really carefully. What did you say about the music?"

The alien paused, suddenly feeling more than a little intimidated by Jake who was giving off the vibe of someone ten thousand years less removed than he was from being a wild creature killing to survive. "Well..." he said a bit meekly, coming to the conclusion he may have underestimated his opponent and that while some diplomacy wouldn't hurt him the being in front of him just might.

"It sucks!" said a different alien in the back who wasn't close enough to pick up on the sudden primeval aura hanging in the air.

"That's what I thought you said," said Jake, rearing back and sending a hard right fist into the chin of the alien in front of him as Steve leapt from his chair to back up his friend for the twelfth time. Robb bounced clear over the table and onto the head and shoulders of one of the aliens, little fists flying while Johnny circled around trying to decide if the enemy's family jewels were likely to be where he thought they should be.

Varcus sighed a big sigh. "Oh hell," he said and got up and picked up one of the aliens and tossed him halfway across the room.

Larry stood and puffed out his chest and chin, smiled a gigantic smile and threw all four arms open wide. "Battle!" he cried happily and launched himself into the fray.

Chapter Twenty-Five

"Dude, I can't believe they threw us off the planet," said Johnny as they cruised through space past the planet Trius of the Kador solar system.

"It's getting to be a kind of a trend isn't it?" said Steve.

"We sure showed those guys though didn't we?" said Jake.

"It didn't hurt we had the purple Hercules on our side," said Steve who was feeling a bit calmer this voyage now that he was a seasoned astronaut and Varcus had left the dome of the ship up.

"You were like a weed whacker, Robodude," said Johnny, reunited with his skateboard at last and fondling it fondly.

"It sort of helped my simulation circuits were off and I couldn't feel any pain," said Robb.

"Did you see that thing Larry did with his guy's left elbow and right ear? Ouch." said Jake.

Steve stretched. "Ouch is right though. I'm pretty sore today."

"Yeah, a couple of them got in some good licks on me too," said Jake. "But at least we don't all have hangovers on top of it. Those pills Varcus gave us did wonders. And I gotta say that was the nicest jail I've ever been in. I've been in hotel rooms with more uncomfortable beds."

"It was a lot better than the one I was in on Earth the night before," said Robb who was now an almost seasoned enough ex-con to start composing Johnny Cash songs.

A door opened and Varcus walked into the room. "Jake, we need to talk."

"Yeah, I know. I'm sorry about last night," said Jake.

"Last night? Oh that. Don't worry about it. They had it coming," said Varcus.

"You're not mad?" asked Steve.

"No, why should I be?" said Varcus.

"Then you didn't get into any trouble for it?" asked Jake.

"Not yet. It'll be coming sooner or later though so at least I've got something to look forward to," said Varcus.

"I didn't hear. Did they ban you from Kador for a year too?" asked Jake.

"Again not yet, mostly because I'm a government official of sorts," said Varcus. "They banned Larry of course, but then they do that about once a year anyway."

"Good old Larry," said Jake, who had managed to grow a bit fonder of him now that they had bonded in the fire of combat.

"Well, good old Larry is what I wanted to talk to you about," said Varcus. "I just got off the phone with Verice my ancestral half-cousin three hundred and seventy-eight times removed on my mother's side. She cocktails in the lounge on space station Robeela and she said Larry was in there last week and told her some very interesting things before they threw him off the station. Do you guys know for instance why he wants to move you to Aurora?"

"So he'll finally have some friends?" suggested Steve.

"No but that's a good guess," said Varcus.

"I thought it was because he wanted pizza," said Jake.

166

"You're right he does. In fact he wants it so bad he's bringing you to the planet just so he can open a pizza parlor," said Varcus. "A really big pizza parlor."

"Like how big?" asked Jake.

"Big enough to serve the galaxy," said Varcus.

"That's pretty big," agreed Jake.

"Yes it will cover a good portion of the planet. Larry plans to use the same displacement technology we use on our space ships to transport piping hot pizzas to hungry aliens everywhere," said Varcus. "And he's going to use your people to grow the ingredients and bake them. He hopes to make a bundle."

"And he doesn't want free pizza?" said Steve.

"No he definitely wants that too," said Varcus.

"And if we get to Aurora and simply refuse to go along with his evil plan?" said Jake.

"Then he can make you do what he wants by pointing a ray or two at you," said Varcus.

"What, you guys have a ray that'll turn is all into Chef Boyardees?" asked Steve.

"No, but Larry could use one that makes you all vulnerable to suggestions," said Varcus. "The practice is definitely frowned upon, but Aurora is a privately owned planet so no one could interfere."

"And you're sure about all this?" asked Jake.

"I'm afraid so," said Varcus. "He even offered to bring Verice back to his ship and show her his pizza pie charts."

167

"Boy if that isn't the oldest line in the book," said Jake. "You know he better hope he's not around when I get back to Earth."

A ship's buzzer sounded three times. "Which will be in just a couple of moments," said Varcus. "I have to get back to the bridge and land us," he said and left the room.

Steve came over to Jake. "So what are you going to do?"

"What am I going to do?" said Jake. "Let's just say Larry and I are going to have a little chat when we get back to your nice, quiet farm. Just he and I. Alone."

Chapter Twenty-Six

Jake stepped out of Varcus' ship and onto the ramp and a sea of flashbulbs went off in his face. He blinked and waited for the spots to clear out of his eyes then opened them and found a crowd of aliens of all sizes, shapes and colors milling about the pasture and yard. He stared at them in disbelief for a moment then walked down the ramp followed by Steve who pushed his way through the crowd towards the house, anxious to see his new bride.

A pudgy creature wearing a flowered shirt and a hat with a feather in it walked up to Jake and held up a picture and compared it to him. "That's him! That's the Representative," he said and another wave of flashes popped off.

"Ooh! The Representative!" said a tall blue alien with three eyes.

"Take my picture with it!" said a yellow and red spotted creature with wings.

A slimy looking alien covered in moving fungus held out an equally slimy looking book. "Can I have your autograph?"

"What the hell is going on here?" said Jake. "Who are all you things, uh, people?"

"Oh, sorry," said the pudgy alien. "Din Weeber. Sun Planet tours," he said, then pointed to a gaudy looking ship resembling a tour bus painted with stars, comets and planets that was parked in the street.

"What are you all doing here?" asked Jake.

"Touring your planet. Seeing you and your people in their natural habitat before you're not in it anymore," explained Din.

"This is not good. Cynthia is not going to like this," said Jake.

"Look, mammal excretions," said a three legged alien. "Take a picture of me with them."

"Remember, folks, it's against interstellar customs regulations to remove anything from an undeveloped planet, doomed inhabitants or otherwise," shouted Din into an electronic megaphone.

A dignified voice came from behind Jake. "Pardon me, but you are the Representative aren't you?"

Jake turned and found a very green eight foot tall plant being covered in little orange colored blossoms addressing him. "Yeah, that's what everyone keeps telling me," said Jake, now at the point where nothing came as a shock anymore.

"If you have a moment I would like to talk to you about the future of the plant life here on Earth," said the plant. "I know as a mammal you probably overlook the well being of vegetation but if you could just hear me out..."

"Look, I don't have time for this," said Jake. "The only plant I give a hoot about is the potted fern in my living room and he's perfectly safe."

"If you really cared about him you would set him free so he could frolic in the wild," said the plant.

"I don't think he's much into frolicking but I'll ask him the next chance I get," said Jake, looking around for someplace else to be. "Now beat it before I go looking for Steve's Weed-B-Gone."

The plant creature managed to look scared and moved quickly off.

"Quite a mess isn't it?" asked Varcus who had come out of the ship to see what he could do to help.

"What is that thing anyway?" said Jake, pointing at the plant creature who was bending down to shake hands with a not so innocent dandelion.

"A Chrysanthaman," said Varcus. "Pollinated too. He'll be bearing fruit in a few weeks."

"That's probably all I want to know about that," said Jake. He looked over and saw that Larry's ship was back and spied him near it talking to two curvaceous orange tourists and stomped towards him, Varcus following. "Hey, Larry! I want to talk to you!"

The two identically attractive tangerine creatures moved off. "Well I hope this is important," said Larry sadly, watching them leave. "You chased off the twins."

"They're all twins, you moron," said Varcus.

"What do you mean?" said Larry.

"Go to Olandal some time. It's inhabitants are all identical," said Varcus.

Larry considered this. "That could be most fun," he said thoughtfully.

"Including the males and females," said Varcus. "They're impossible to tell apart, even for Olandals."

"Hmm. I'll have to consider that further. The potential for extremely embarrassing situations might outweigh the potential for quintuple horizontal mamboing."

said Larry. "Anyway, what did you want, Jake? I suppose since Varcus moves you tomorrow morning you're finally ready to take me up on my gallant offer?"

"Well you suppose wrong," snapped Jake. "Varcus passed on some information from one of his sources and I can tell you right now there's no way the human race is going to spend eternity tossing dough for you."

Larry thought for a moment. "Verice! I hate how every Vandorian is related."

"Yes we are, and stop hitting on my cousins," said Varcus.

"I can't help it. I have a weakness for tall, dark and violet women," said Larry.

"You know you have some nerve trying to trick these people," said Varcus.

"Hey at least I'm not moving them to some hole and giving their home to a race of annoying little twerps," said Larry.

"What?!" said Jake.

"Well--" said Varcus. "Perhaps I should explain."

"Perhaps you should. Do you mean to tell me you have someone else moving onto the Earth?" said Jake.

"Yes, I admit I do. The Kapaloo. Their world is doomed you see," said Varcus.

"Why should they get our home just because their own planet is doomed?" said Jake.

"Because unlike your people they're not the ones who doomed it," said Varcus.

Nicole walked up to Jake. "Welcome home, Jake. What's going on?"

172

"The purple people mover here gave our planet to another species and didn't think it was important enough to tell us," said Jake.

"You still have Aurora to fall back on," said Larry. "Sandy beaches, champagne wishes and caviar dreams."

"And spending the rest of my life on the phone asking if some space hamster wants thin or thick crust? No thank you," said Jake.

A short, bookworm looking little alien with spectacles tugged on Jake's shirt hem. "Can I have a lock of your hair mister alien?"

"Hey! No DNA samples!" said Din, and he rushed over and guided the creature away.

"But I just wanted to clone him when I got home," protested the nerdling.

"I can't take much more of this," said Jake.

Steve came out of the house with a cell phone in his hand and shouted across the yard at Jake. "Hey, Jake!"

"Hey, what?!" shouted Jake back.

"The President is on the phone," said Steve.

"Which one?" said Jake.

"The one," said Steve.

"Oh that one," said Jake. "About time! Maybe I'm finally gonna get some help around here."

"I don't think so," said Steve. "He and the First Lady are packing and they just want to know if they should bring their bathing suits."

"That does it!" said Jake, exasperated. "I've had it. I didn't ask for any of this. I'm done dealing with it. Move us, keep us here, make us slice pepperoni, I don't care anymore!"

He looked around then walked off towards the back of the property.

"Jake, where are you going?" asked Nicole.

"Away," said Jake without turning.

"You can't walk off the planet you know," said Larry.

Nicole started to follow but Varcus put out his hand to stop her. "Better let him be dear."

Nicole watched Jake go then shook her head and walked towards the house and Larry moved over next to Varcus.

"Well I hope you're happy," said Larry eventually as Jake went out of sight.

"Shut up," said Varcus.

Chapter Twenty-Seven

Jake sat on a grassy hill on the edge of a small bluff that overlooked the farm. It was near sunset, the sky turning every shade of red and gold it could think of. Insects and little dandelion puffs floated around Jake in the light evening breeze. He stared out into the distance, his knees up and his arms resting upon them as Nicole walked towards him.

"There you are," said Nicole. "I've been looking everywhere for you."

"Yep. Here I am," said Jake, still gazing off into the distance.

"We were all worried about you," said Nicole.

"Just needed to be by myself for a while," said Jake.

"Would you like me to leave?" asked Nicole.

Jake finally looked at her. "No. Have a seat," he said and she sat down next to him. "The alien paparazzi still down there?"

"No, Cynthia came out on the porch with a shotgun and fired off a couple of warning shots and they cleared out in a hurry," said Nicole.

"That's my girl. I'm beginning to understand what Steve sees in her," said Jake.

"So what happened down there?" Nicole asked.

"I don't know. All of a sudden it hit me what was going on and it was just too big," said Jake.

"I suppose it's not very fair you having to deal with all this," said Nicole.

"That's just the thing though," said Jake. "I thought about it and it is fair. As fair as it being anyone else anyway."

"What do you mean?" said Nicole.

"I mean I'm just as guilty as the next civilized human when it comes to the planet's environment," said Jake. "It would be unfair if it was some pygmy from a lost tribe that had been served. He'd wonder what the hell he did to deserve it. But I'm not exactly mister green jeans either you know. Yeah I throw a can in the recycle bin from time to time. But other than that it's all about whatever works for me. I just want to crank up the air conditioning then hop in my car, drive a few blocks, get out and buy a bunch of stuff and consume. Maybe stop on the way home and get a burger made from an ecologically unfriendly cow. But is that worth losing all this?" said Jake, pointing at the vista all around them. "It's beautiful isn't it?"

"Yes it is," said Nicole.

"I just wish I'd paid more attention to it before," said Jake. "Maybe nothing would have changed but at least I'd have spent more time enjoying it."

"You know, Jake, in our defense we have made life better. Can you imagine how hard things were a thousand years ago?" said Nicole.

"I know. We just didn't know when to stop," said Jake.

"I guess you're right," said Nicole.

"The more I think about it the more I wonder if we shouldn't just go along quietly to Gork. Give the poor Earth a break. At least we'd be saving the Pakaloons," said Jake.

"Maybe," said Nicole.

There was a long quiet moment as Jake and Nicole sat soaking up their surroundings.

"We should be getting back soon," said Nicole finally.

"Yeah. But not yet," said Jake.

"Okay. Not yet," said Nicole, and she leaned over and put her head on Jake's shoulder.

Chapter Twenty-Eight

"Steve!" shouted Cynthia. "Would you get in here? You're going to miss it."

"I think this is one flight you can't miss," said Nicole.

Steve rushed into the living room holding up a box of matches then put them into his backpack. "Suddenly remembered *Cast Away*," he said. "I'm not very good at rubbing sticks together."

"Yeah I get the feeling I'm going to regret being the only person in America who didn't watch Survivor," said Jake. He looked around the room. "So where do you guys think? Right here okay?"

Steve looked up. "I'm thinking outside. I don't know how this is gonna work but I really don't want to go up through the roof if I don't have to."

"Good point. Outside it is," said Jake.

The four of them picked up their bags and walked outside then went over to an open area of grass devoid of trees near the two space ships. Larry, who was sitting in a chair outside of his ship, came over to talk to them. "Are you sure you don't want to change your mind? Making pizza is a noble profession and the tips would be good," he said.

"No thanks. I might get used to being a slave but I'd get so sick and tired of pizza that I'd never want to eat it again and that I couldn't live with," said Jake.

"Well it's your decision. Personally I think you're not looking at the big picture but then again the picture in this case is quite humongous so perhaps it will take your eyes some time to critique it all," said Larry. "I'll stop in and visit you on Gork and maybe you'll have finished your viewing by then."

"You do that," said Jake.

Larry walked back to his ship and the four friends stood waiting.

"Do you think this is going to hurt?" asked Nicole.

"Naw," said Jake. "They're just going to suck us off the planet into ships miles away up in space, probably tearing every molecule in our bodies apart before slamming them all back together again. Why should it hurt?"

"Thanks for making me feel better," said Nicole.

"Don't mention it," said Jake.

They waited for a while in the midst of yet another in the string of beautiful days the Earth had kicked out lately as if it was showing everyone what they were going to be missing.

"I'm going to miss all this," said Steve, reading the Earth's message loud and clear.

"Me too," said Jake.

"Maybe Gork won't be as bad as it sounds," said Nicole.

"Maybe," said Jake. "Or maybe it will be a lot worse and they just didn't want to scare us."

"You know you're just a ray of sunshine today," said Nicole.

Everyone stood holding their bags and waited some more, this more seeming quite long. "Does anyone have a watch?" asked Cynthia finally. "My arms are getting tired."

"No," said Nicole and Jake together.

"Yeah I didn't see the point either with the shorter days on Gork," said Steve. " I'd have to reset the thing every nine hours."

They waited a short bit longer.

"Are we there--" began Jake, but he was interrupted as the four of them disappeared from the Earth accompanied by a strange, wet popping sound like a big finger coming out of a mouth.

They reappeared inside a transport ship with four more popping sounds, followed very quickly by hundreds of other people in an avalanche of wet pops. Everyone was squeezed together in the dull, grey, dingy hold which was lit by strips of yellow lighting running around the ceiling where it met with the walls.

"--yet?" finished Jake.

The group looked around them.

"Welcome to transport ship 2738-A," said a robotic sounding voice over a loud speaker. "Please remain standing for the duration of the trip."

"And I thought coach was bad," said Nicole. "This is going to be a long flight."

"Thank you for your cooperation," said the voice a second or so later. "And welcome to Gork."

"You were saying?" said Jake, unsurprised and well versed in space travel times.

"We can't be there al--" began Nicole before vanishing in a pop.

"--ready," said Nicole as she reappeared on the surface of Gork alongside Jake, Steve and Cynthia as other people from the Annandale area arrived in the distance in a barrage of pops.

Jake dropped his bags and looked around him.

"Man, we are so doomed," said Steve.

"For once I agree with you," said Jake.

The four friends finally saw Gork for the first time. It was a dark place. The sky was filled with sickly green and yellow swirling clouds while the ground was made up of brown, black and grey dirt and rock. Black wooded trees with dark leaves grew scattered about. Yellow scrub bushes stuck out of the ground and orange moss grew on many of the stones. Odd noises seemed to come from everywhere, some like animals or birds but others indefinable. The wind made an annoying off key whistling sound.

Everyone began to sweat immediately in the intense heat as Nicole snapped a picture of the planet. "I don't know," she said. "It could be worse. Couldn't it?"

"Not unless we were already dead instead of soon to be dead," said Steve, just seconds before a snarling, growling sound came from somewhere on the ground behind him.

Steve froze and Jake looked down to see what was making the noise that had sent a chill down his spine in the one hundred degree plus heat. "Uh, Steve? You were saying something about soon being dead?" asked Jake.

"What is that, Jake?" asked Steve, doing his best to imitate a rock.

"If I had to name it I'd call it fangs with feet," said Jake.

"What should I do?" said Steve.

"Run," said Jake and Nicole together.

Steve looked down behind him and yelped, then dropped his bags and took off running as fast as he could as an ugly creature about three feet long with a single small eye and a large mouthful of teeth above six legs chased after him, snarling as it went.

"Steve!" shrieked Cynthia, dropping her belongings and running after them.

"Well they'll be busy for a while," said Jake matter-of-factly. "Damn it's hot," he added, wiping the sweat off his brow.

"They said it was going to be hot," said Nicole.

"No, they said it was going to be hot," said Jake. "This isn't hot. I've been in hot before, and this makes hot seem cool. I mean I'm going to have to come up a new word for this hot."

Nicole saw something and pointed. "What are those?" she asked, taking a picture.

Jake looked over at the tall tree at which Nicole was pointing. In it sat two very large bird like creatures, about five feet or so tall. They looked almost like giant vultures but had a single eye and ratty fur instead of feathers. The beasts gazed down at the people who had just arrived with interest.

"I don't know but I hope they don't decide to make us part of the local food chain," said Jake.

A small silver robot with spindly arms and a TV screen for a face flew up to them. "Greetings, and welcome to Gork," it said, the words simultaneously scrolling across it's screen. "I am an orientation bot. Please pick out a shelter

182

to live in. A shower and restroom facility is located in the center of your designated area alongside a mess hall where delicious food and water can be found. Sustenance will be provided for six Gorkian months. After that you are on your own. Do you have any questions?"

"I do," said Nicole. "Where are all the other humans? I just see the same townspeople I saw in Annandale."

"That is probably because your species has been placed on Gork in as close a relation as possible to where you were picked up on Earth. It would appear you came from a sparsely populated area," explained the robot.

"So a few hundred miles to the east there are about ten million people all crammed together?" said Jake.

"If you mean the citizens of the Chicago-Milwaukee metropolitan area then yes," said the robot.

"Wow. We lucked out there," said Jake.

"I'll say," said Nicole.

The robot buzzed off to greet other people.

"You know, I feel kind of light," said Nicole, moving up and down on her heels and toes.

"Me too. Like I have a new pair of sneaks on," said Jake. He jumped up and down a little and liked what he felt, then crouched and jumped as high as he could. He shot up about ten feet off the ground and came back down, landing a bit clumsily. "That was crazy," he said. "The gravity must be lower here. Look, I can be like Mike."

Jake spent the next few minutes bouncing merrily around the area imitating Michael Jordan as Nicole watched. Finally she yawned and said "Well, this is fun but I'm going to go check out the shelters."

Jake landed reluctantly back on the surface. "Wait, I'll go with you."

They managed to pick up their and Steve and Cynthia's bags and lugged them over to the nearest shelter. It was an institutional green plastic looking building which was shaped more or less like a cheap small house. Jake knocked on a wall as if to test it, then Nicole opened the door and she and Jake went inside. The room they entered was a common area with doors leading off to other rooms. Block shaped chairs, benches and tables were molded into the floor. Light filtered in through screened windows.

"I wish I would have brought some magazines with me," said Jake, looking the room over. "I'm gonna need something to read if I'm going to live in a giant porta potty." He looked into one of the four side rooms which turned out to be a sleeping area with a single molded bed complete with foam mattress and tossed his bags inside. He found another room with two such beds and put Steve and Cynthia's luggage into it. "This setup is really going to put a cramp in the newlywed's style. Hey, you want to stay here too?"

"Why, Jake. Are you asking me too move in with you?" asked Nicole, batting her eyelashes at him.

"I'm asking you to grab one of those last two rooms before some weirdo takes them," said Jake.

"I don't know," said Nicole thoughtfully. "I should probably try and find my parents."

"You sure you want to walk halfway across an alien planet to New Milwaukee?" he said.

"Good point," said Nicole, and she put her things into a room.

184

"Cool. Now we just have to find one more roomie," said Jake.

Nicole looked around her. "Well it's not much but I guess it'll keep us dry."

A tap came on the roof of their new home followed quickly by two, then three then eight more. They multiplied quickly and noisily on the hard plastic-like surface, growing louder and louder until Jake and Nicole had to yell to at one another to hear.

"What the hell is that?" shouted Jake, hands over his ears.

"I think it's rain." Nicole yelled back.

"I'd rather be wet than deaf. Come on," said Jake, heading towards the door.

They rushed outside and almost ran into Johnny who was carrying a couple of huge bags and his skateboard. "Repman! Dude, are you guys living in there?"

"Umm..." said Jake.

"Cool, dude. I was looking for a place to live. My mom said it was a good time for me to finally move out of her house. You've got space don't ya?" said Johnny.

"Well, yeah but--" said Jake.

"You don't mind, do you?" Johnny asked Nicole.

"Um...well," said Nicole.

"Awesome. I'll just put my stuff inside," said Johnny before going through the door.

Jake and Nicole stood looking at one another in the rain as if the other they were looking at should have done something about the new wrinkle in their housing situation but were quickly distracted by a sudden assault on their olfactory senses.

Jake sniffed the air and Nicole crinkled her nose. "What the hell is that smell?" asked Jake.

"I don't know but it's awful," said Nicole.

Jake sniffed all around him, then smelled Nicole and recoiled in disgust. "Damn! What perfume are you wearing, girl, essence of boiled cabbage?"

Nicole smelled herself. "Ugh. It's not me, it's the rain."

Jake caught some in his hand and took a whiff and almost gagged. "Dats just great," he said, holding his nose shut.

Steve came running up to them and stopped, bending over and putting his hands on his knees to rest, fully out of breath.

"Got away from that thing huh? Still got all your body parts?" said Jake.

Steve nodded and Jake looked around.

"Hey, where's Cynthia?" asked Jake, worried. "That creature didn't--"

"No, she's fine," panted Steve. "She ducked into the mess hall when the rain started."

"How do you know it was the mess hall?" asked Nicole.

"Because of the big mess hall sign on it," said Steve. "Are we all living in there?" he asked, pointing at the shelter.

"Yeah, we put your bags inside," said Jake.

"Thanks," said Steve, finally able to stand up.

A loud rolling sound came from inside the shelter.

"What's that noise?" asked Steve.

"That would be your new roommate skateboarding around the living room," said Nicole.

"Johnny's in there? Who said he could live with us?" asked Steve.

Jake and Nicole pointed at one another.

"What the hell. No point in going half-assed about it, might as well be totally miserable," said Steve. "Come on, let's get out of this rain. I'll show you the way to the mess hall."

The three of them headed towards a very large plastic building in the center of all the shelters. Steve opened the door for Nicole and she went inside.

"You know a few days of this place and I'll be ready to go extinct," said Steve.

"I'll be right behind you," said Jake.

"You think that's what happened to the dinosaurs?" said Steve.

"What, the planet annoyed them to death? I don't think the Earth was ever this bad, even the parts without cable. Come on, let's see what's for lunch," said Jake and he slapped Steve on the back as they went inside.

Chapter Twenty-Nine

Jake, Nicole, Steve, Cynthia and Johnny sat on a circle of large rocks around a campfire Steve had built. It was night, the clouded Gorkian sky fading to a dark gloomy starless veil.

"Well, we made it through our first day on Gork," said Steve.

"Steve. We've been here six hours," said Jake.

"Still," said Steve.

"Wow, dinner like totally sucked didn't it?" said Johnny.

"It might be a little more palatable if it didn't come out of a big vat labeled human food," said Nicole.

"That was kind of a turn off," said Jake. "And I hope the name doesn't mean what it tasted like it means."

"Well I have a surprise for everyone," said Steve. He reached behind him and got his backpack and pulled out a box of graham crackers, a bag of marshmallows and a bag of mini Hershey bars. "Ta-da!"

"Steve! You remembered the smores this time!" said Jake.

"I thought we might all need a treat on our first night," said Steve. He grabbed some sticks he had collected and handed them out, then passed around the marshmallows. Soon everyone was roasting them over the fire, smiling at doing a simple Earth pleasure.

"Thanks, Steve," said Johnny.

"Yeah, man. Good thinking," said Jake.

"That's my hubby," said Cynthia.

"And happy honeymoon, you two," said Jake.

"Wow. Almost forgot about that," said Steve.

"Hey!" said Cynthia, slapping Steve on the arm.

"Umm. This is good," said Nicole around a mouth full of smores.

"Yeah all we need now is a case of cold beer," said Jake.

"I'll see what I can do, bro," said Johnny.

"Yeah right. What are you gonna do, skateboard down to the local liquor store?" said Steve.

"Don't worry man, I got it covered," said Johnny.

"Good. Then stop at McDonalds on the way back and pick up some Big Macs," said Jake.

Everyone laughed except for Johnny.

"Duuuuudes," said Johnny, hurt at the lack of confidence.

"And don't forget the fries," said Nicole.

"Or the hot apple pies," said Cynthia.

"Dudes! Where is the trust?" said Johnny.

Chapter Thirty (Two Gorkian weeks later)

Tommy stood on the mound and shook off the sign from Steve. Then he shook it off again. And again. And again.

"Would you just pitch it already? It's underhand softball for crying out loud!" said Steve.

"Just trying to add a little drama," said Tommy.

"Squatting here in this heat is drama enough," said Steve.

Tommy went into his windup and tossed the softball and it arced gracefully towards home plate until Jake's bat intercepted it and sent it sailing high into the angry Gorkian sky and far off into the distance.

"Dammit, Jake!" complained Craig who was playing first base.

"Oops! My bad," said Jake.

"Who's going to go get it this time?" asked Steve. A low, menacing growl came from behind him and he sighed. "Never mind, I got it," he said and tossed his glove to Jake then took off running in the direction the ball had gone, Fangfeet right on his heels for the fourteenth day in a row.

"Hey, Jake," said Tommy, motioning behind him. Jake turned and found Varcus standing nearby with a five foot tall, very thin furry red alien. The being had long, pointy ears and resembled an ugly kangaroo.

"Varcus! What are you doing here? Come to see if we messed up Gork yet?" said Jake. "Although I don't know how you'd be able to tell."

"Hello, Jake. No, I'm here because I need to talk to you," said Varcus.

Jake dropped his bat and Steve's glove on the ground and walked over. "Okay. We have to wait for the ball to come back anyway. I keep forgetting to lighten up on my swing in this low gravity."

"Jake, this is Qwas. He's one of the Kapaloos, the race that was moving to the Earth," said Varcus.

"Hey. Jake Williams, Representative," said Jake and he put out his hand to shake, but Qwas looked at it as if he'd been offered a decaying fish.

"Sorry, I make it a point to avoid contact with primitive alien creatures," said Qwas in an annoying nasally voice. "You never know where they've been."

"Suit yourself," said Jake. "Let's head over to my office."

They walked away from the makeshift field towards a large gas grill where Mark was cooking. A table next to him was covered with bowls filled with baked beans, chips and dips.

"How do you want your steak, Jake?" asked Mark.

"Medium rare," said Jake.

"You got it. Hello, Varcus," said Mark.

Varcus looked puzzled. "You have steaks?"

Jake grabbed a handful of chips and started munching on them. "Yeah. Someone must have brought 'um from Earth."

"And the grill?" asked Varcus.

"I guess someone brought that too," said Jake.

Varcus looked unconvinced but said nothing and they continued walking until they came to a green metal cooler under a big beach umbrella. Jake opened it and pulled a frosty bottle out of the ice. "You guys want a cold beer?"

"No!" said Varcus irritably.

"Ack! Certainly not," said Qwas.

Jake shrugged and opened the bottle and took a long drink. "Ahh," he said. "You guys don't know what you're missing. Nothing like a frosty brew on a fine Gorkian day."

"Alright, Jake, what's going on?" said Varcus.

"What do you mean?" said Jake innocently.

"You know exactly what I mean!" said Varcus. "Where'd all this stuff come from? The grill, steaks, beer...and ice? Where in Kelgrin did you get manage to find ice on this planet? And don't tell me somebody brought it."

"How else would we get it?" asked Jake. "How many humans have you see cruising around in space? Other than me, Steve and Johnny of course and those trudges NASA took to the moon."

"Well none but--" said Varcus.

"Then I guess we must have brought it all with us," said Jake.

"It's Larry, isn't it? I bet these are all bribes from him aren't they?" said Varcus.

"No, but if they were I'd gladly accept them. We need all the help we can get," said Jake. "Larry is around here somewhere though with a petition to try and get me to move everyone to Aurora. I told him I'd consider it if he got four billion signatures."

"Four billion?" said Varcus.

"Yeah it should keep him out of my hair for a few days," said Jake.

"Ola, Varcus dude!" said Johnny as he walked by. "How's my main metal man Robb Ott?"

"More rebellious than ever," said Varcus. "Someday I'd like to know what you did to him."

"Just played him some tunes man," said Johnny.

"I had no idea Earth music was so dangerous," said Varcus.

"Only when it's done right," said Johnny.

"How's the skate park coming, Johnny?" asked Jake.

"Almost done, dude. The cement should be dry by tomorrow," said Johnny.

"Sweeeeeet," said Jake.

Johnny waved goodbye and wandered off to do whatever it was he did every day.

"Cement?" said Varcus. "I suppose you're going to tell me that someone brought that too."

Jake looked innocent again and Varcus sighed.

"Fine. Be that way. But I will get to the bottom of it," said Varcus.

"You do that," said Jake.

Varcus opened his mouth to say something but stopped and looked off to his left, puzzled. "Jake, who are all those people?"

Jake looked over and found a group of miserable, sweaty looking humans staring angrily back at him.

"Oh them. Just ignore 'em. I do," said Jake.

"But who are they?" asked Varcus.

"They're my fan club from New Glenbrook," said Jake. "They blame me for this whole Gork thing but since you still have that pacifist ray aimed at us they can't do anything about it so they just come over here every day and give me dirty looks."

"Oh my," said Varcus.

"I'm getting used to it. But I am a little worried what's going to happen when you turn the thing off," said Jake. "So how are you Poopaloos liking the Earth? Did you re-carve Mount Rushmore yet?"

"Kapaloos. And you filthy beings should be ashamed of yourselves," said Qwas. "A nice planet like that and you refused to take care of it."

"Hey, you want to tone down the attitude a bit or are you looking to take part in an intergalactic incident right here and now?" said Jake, who had found that for some reason since going to Kador he seemed to be unaffected by the pacifist ray.

"What kind of intergalactic incident?" said Qwas.

"The kind where I reach out and yank on those stupid looking ears of yours so hard they'll be dragging on the ground," said Jake.

"Ack!" said Qwas.

"Boys..." said Varcus.

Steve came jogging up, totally out of breath but by now in the best shape of his life.

"Larry was right. They are annoying little twerps," said Jake.

"Huh?" said Steve, panting.

"Did you get the ball?" asked Jake.

"Yes and no. I found it and grabbed it on the run while that little s.o.b. was chasing me then I ran back towards the field. I tried to throw it to Mark but I forgot about the gravity and it sailed off over his head," explained Steve. "Funny thing is Fangfeet took off after it."

"Can we get back to what I came here to talk to you about?" said Varcus "We have a bit of a problem."

"We? In case you haven't noticed *we* already have a problem of our own so I'm not sure we want anything to do with this new one of yours," said Jake.

"When the Kapaloo advance team came down to check out the Earth they began sneezing and all their hair fell out," said Varcus. "And if there's one thing you don't want to see it's naked, hairless Kapaloos. No offense."

"Ack! " said Qwas.

"Wow I feel real sorry for them," said Jake. "So what's wrong? Are they allergic to peanut butter and strawberries or something?"

"No, to the sky," said Varcus.

"The sky? What you mean like oxygen, nitrogen that kind of thing?" asked Steve.

"No the color," said Varcus.

"Come again," said Jake.

"It turns out the Kapaloo are allergic to the color blue, at least in large quantities or close proximity," said Varcus. "There's no blue on their home world. They can't even see it. The Earth sky just looked blank to them. We had a devil of a time trying to figure out what was wrong with them."

"That's the stupidest thing I've ever heard, and I've heard some whoppers in the last couple of weeks," said Jake. "Hey, Steve, give me your shirt."

Steve peeled off his light blue sweat drenched t-shirt and tossed it to Jake.

"This is definitely all bull shit," said Jake. He held the shirt out very close to Qwas and the creature sneezed extremely hard, his fur flying off in every direction.

"Okay, maybe not," said Jake.

Qwas stood and tried to cover himself. "That's just perfect," he said irritably.

"And I was sure you couldn't get any uglier," said Jake.

"Now do you believe me?" said Varcus.

Jake smelled the shirt. "Phew! I don't know, Steve's deodorant gave out about a week ago I think. If I had to smell his shirt too many times my hair would probably fall out too."

"Trust me, it's the color," said Varcus.

"So can't you just give them all sunglasses or something?" said Jake.

"It wouldn't help. The sky would still be there," said Varcus.

"Looks like you do have a problem. Wish I could help," said Jake.

"Glad to hear you say that Jake," said Varcus.

"Oh you thought I meant that?" said Jake.

Fangfeet came jogging up to Steve, the softball lodged firmly between his chompers. He deposited it at Steve's feet and stood growling at him, jaws open, mouth drooling and

196

tail wagging. Steve gingerly reached out and picked up the slimy mutilated remains of the ball and threw it way off into the distance and Fangfeet snarled happily and charged off after it.

"What do you know. All this time he just wanted to play," said Steve.

"Look, this will help you and your people too, Jake," said Varcus. "Since there's no blue to be found anywhere on Gork we've decided to move the Kapaloos here instead."

"So are you putting us back on Earth then?" asked Jake hopefully.

"No, but we can move you to Dacoola Five. It's a bit nicer than Gork, more temperate. A class C planet. Gork is a D. It will still be difficult but your people will have a much better chance of survival there."

"That's great news, isn't it Jake?" said Steve, but Jake didn't respond and stood with his head down, thinking. "Jake?"

"Uh-uh," said Jake.

"Uh-uh? Uh-uh as in it's not great news?" said Steve.

"Uh-uh as in I think we'll just stay right here," said Jake.

"Are you crazy?" said Steve. "This planet is a dump. Anywhere is better than here."

"I don't know, I kind of like it. Besides, Johnny just finished his skateboard park," said Jake.

"Look, it's not like you have a lot of say in the matter," said Varcus.

"Oh don't I? I'm still the Representative right? We haven't messed up Gork yet, have we?" said Jake.

"Well yes and yes but--" said Varcus.

"Then I'm thinking you can't move us unless I say it's alright and we can stay put if we want to," said Jake.

"Yes but *we* don't want to," said Steve.

Nicole and Larry came walking up to the group, Nicole looking for some back up in the face of yet another of Larry's advances. "What's going on?" she asked.

"Jake's finally gone insane in the heat," said Steve. Nicole leaned close to him and he quietly brought her up to speed.

"You're being difficult for no good reason, Jake. The Kapaloo can't survive on Earth and their home world will soon be uninhabitable," said Varcus.

"Then I guess they're screwed aren't they? Unless you want to put us back on the Earth," said Jake.

"You know I can't do that," said Varcus.

"This is all your fault!" screeched Qwas shrilly.

"My fault?" said Varcus.

"You're the one that sold us that planet," said Qwas.

"Sold it? You didn't mention any money being involved. No wonder you were so anxious to move us," said Jake.

"I didn't make a profit from it," said Varcus. "Most of the funds went to pay for moving all of you around. The rest went into the planetary protection fund."

"It doesn't matter! You sold us a planet we can't live on!" complained Qwas.

"I am sorry, but you passed all the compatibility tests and signed the papers," said Varcus.

"You should have been more thorough!" said Qwas.

"There's nothing I can do now," said Varcus.

"You know there is, Varcus," said Jake. "We'll be glad to hand Gork over to you and the Krapaloons. Just put us back where we belong."

"You belong here. Or on some other planet. But not on Earth. Not anymore," said Varcus.

"Well I guess you're in a tight spot then aren't you? Because it looks like they aren't too happy," said Jake.

"Yes, I'd sue you if I was them," said Larry.

"Ack! We would too, but we ate all our lawyers," said Qwas.

"We've got some we could loan you if you promise not to eat them," said Jake.

"You have lawyers?" said Qwas.

"Thousands and thousands of them," said Jake. "In fact there's one right there!" he said, pointing at Steve and tossing his shirt to him. "Put your clothes on and try to look lawyerly."

Steve put his shirt back on.

"And they would file suit for us?" asked Qwas.

"Now wait a minute!" said Varcus.

"Steve and I would love to. It's what we do," said Jake.

"Actually under interstellar law each plaintiff can have a separate lawyer file a grievance," said Larry.

"One for each lawyer?" said Jake. "What do we have, Steve? About a million attorneys?"

"Probably in the U.S. alone," said Steve.

"You can't do this!" said Varcus.

"Why not?" said Jake.

"Because...because...because for one thing neither one of your races has interstellar travel. You won't even be able to physically file!" said Varcus.

"I have interstellar travel. I'll be glad to do it for them," said Larry.

"Why would you want to do something like that?" said Varcus.

"In exchange for free pizza," said Larry. "And because I know it would irritate you."

Varcus sighed. "Alright. I'll refund the Kapaloo's money. But you humans are staying put!"

"We don't want the money! It won't help us if we're burned to cinders," said Qwas. "We need a planet to live on. Give them back the Earth so we can have Gork!"

"You heard the bald guy," said Jake. "Better do as he says or we'll have you stuck in court for the next ten thousand years. You'll have to time travel just to have the sun shine on your ass again."

Varcus stared angrily at Jake, and Jake stared confidently back.

"Well? What's it going to be, Varcus?" said Jake.

"Fine. Give me a moment. I need to make a call," said Varcus sourly.

"Take your time," said Jake.

Varcus walked some distance away, got out his PED and was soon speaking into it.

"Do you think this is going to work, Jake?" asked Nicole.

"It does seem kind of risky," said Steve.

200

"Look, stop worrying. I have 'em right where I want 'em," said Jake. "It's just like a divorce. They want the condo in Miami but they're not going to get it unless they give us the cabin in Vale."

"Can't we have the condo in Miami instead?" asked Larry. "I need to work on my tan."

"The point is, option one, they'll give us back the Earth and we'll all be as happy as can be, or option two they'll force us to move to this other planet Varcus was talking about and we'll at least be happier than we are now, or option three they'll leave us here on Gork and we'll be totally miserable but hey, that's what we were to begin with," said Jake. "I mean, what's the worst that can happen?"

"I hope you're right," said Nicole.

Varcus put the PED away and walked back over to Jake and friends.

"So?" said Jake.

"So they're immediately convening an emergency session of the Galactic Council," said Varcus. "And then there'll be a vote on the matter."

"To decide if we stay here or go back to Earth?" asked Nicole.

"Yes," said Varcus.

"Good," said Jake.

"Or if they exterminate you to get you out of the way of the Kapaloo," said Varcus.

"I guess you forgot to mention option four in your famous *what's the worst that can happen* speech," said Steve.

"I vote for option four!" said Qwas.

"I wonder how Kapaloos taste best," said Jake. "Beer battered or charbroiled?"

"Ack!" said Qwas.

"Tastes like chicken," said Larry. Everyone looked at him. "Well that's what I heard."

"So how long until we'll know?" asked Nicole.

"It should just be a few moments," said Varcus.

They stood silently waiting for Varcus' PED to beep, an invisible clock ticking off in their heads.

"Anyone want to play *Yahtzee*?" said Larry.

"No!" said everyone, including those creatures that had no idea what he was talking about.

"And get your hands off me," said Nicole.

"Which one?" said Larry.

"All of them," said Nicole.

They waited what seemed like an eternity before Varcus' PED finally went off and he answered it. "So what's the verdict?" he said into it.

"Uh-huh," said Varcus.

"I see," said Varcus. "Really?"

"Are you positive? Okay," said Varcus. "I'll inform everyone and we'll get started on it right away."

"Yes you too. Say *hi* to Mafie and the kids for me. Goodbye," said Varcus and he pushed the end button and put his PED away.

"Well?" asked Jake.

"Well what?" asked Varcus.

"What do you think well what? What did they decide?" said Steve.

"Oh that," said Varcus. "We're moving you all back to Earth of course."

"You are?" said Nicole.

"Well there was really nothing else we could do, was there?" asked Varcus. "We weren't going to let the Kapaloo die and we can't legally move you humans off of Gork without your permission."

"What about option four?" asked Qwas, somewhat disappointed.

"They told me to try that," said Varcus. "They were hoping it would scare you all into backing off. Why, you didn't think we'd actually do it did you?"

"The thought crossed *my* mind yes," said Steve.

"I'm amazed they came to a decision so quickly," said Nicole. "It would have taken months or years in one of our courts."

"But your courts are what did it. It was bad enough we didn't have any options, but no one wanted to tangle with all your lawyers," said Varcus.

"So what happens now?" said Jake.

"First we'll have to put the parts of Washington D.C. we've removed back," said Varcus. "We wouldn't want you to lose any of your government."

"Yeah that'd be a shame," said Jake. "And then?"

"And then we'll start transporting you back to Earth. Probably tomorrow afternoon," said Varcus. "So if you'll excuse me I suddenly have a lot of work to do."

"Cool. Great. Go do your thing then," said Jake. Qwas and Varcus headed towards Varcus' ship. "Hey, will we see you back on Earth?"

"No!" said Qwas.

"Not you, Chihuahua man," said Jake.

"I'll be there," said Varcus and he disappeared behind a row of trees.

"I suppose this means you won't honor the petition now?" asked Larry.

"You suppose right," said Jake.

"Dang it. And I was up to fourteen signatures," said Larry and he wandered off to ask Paula for the umpteenth time if she was ready to forgive him yet.

"Nice going, counselor." said Steve. "You pulled it off after all."

"Yeah I'm impressed," said Nicole.

"He never stood a chance," said Jake. "That'll teach him to mess with a planet full of attorneys. I guess that'll be the end of lawyer jokes back on Earth."

"I wouldn't go that far," said Nicole.

"I'm going to go tell Cynthia the good news," said Steve. "At least I think it's good news. She's been decorating our porta-potty all day. Hopefully she'll still want to move. Oh, and we definitely need to throw a party when we get back to Earth and celebrate."

Steve walked away and Jake stood looking very pleased with himself, then scowled and shouted after him. "Tell them first!" he said, pointing at the crowd from New Glenbrook that were still nearby glaring at Jake. A person in the back of the group suddenly held up a homemade sign that read *Jake Sux!* and waved it around.

"Yeah, I suck now," Jake said loudly to them. "Just wait 'till you're all back on Earth. You'll all be naming babies after me."

"So did I hear there's a party on the horizon?" said Nicole.

"That's the rumor," said Jake.

"Do you suppose there'll be dancing?" said Nicole.

"There might be," said Jake. "Why do you ask?"

"I was thinking I might need a partner," said Nicole.

"It looked to me like you already have one," said Jake.

"Who, Larry? Hmm. I suppose the two extra arms might come in handy during a tango. But I had someone else in mind," said Nicole.

"Anyone I know?" said Jake.

"Just some Representative guy," said Nicole.

"Sounds like a real loser to me," said Jake.

"Actually he's turning out to be okay," said Nicole.

"In what way?" said Jake.

"Well he did save the Earth," said Nicole.

"I thought he saved the humans," said Jake.

"Picky, picky," said Nicole. "Anyway I know a girls got to have her standards, but I think *Hero of the human race* might cut it."

"So a date huh? I don't know, that sounds kind of serious," said Jake.

"It could be serious. You think you could handle that?" said Nicole.

"Maybe," said Jake.

Nicole stood smiling at Jake and he stood smiling back, finally running out of witty remarks.

"Okay, you're going to have to give me some time here because I'm not real used to the idea of just one woman," said Jake.

"One woman?" said Nicole.

"Yeah I was thinking you'd have to be a one woman kind of deal," said Jake. "So if we could just take it real slow so I can get acclimated to the whole concept..."

Nicole put her arms around Jake's neck and kissed him.

"Like that?" asked Nicole.

"I don't know," said Jake. "Are you asking like that as in slow like that or if I liked that? Cause if you're asking if that was a good example of taking it slow I'd have to say no, but if you were asking me if I liked it then the answer would be a really big yes."

Nicole took Jake by the hand and they walked towards the shelters. "Come on. Let's go get packed."

"Yeah, I guess tomorrow afternoon isn't that long from now on this little ball of joy is it?" said Jake.

"Nope," said Nicole. "So do you think Varcus is ever going to figure out Johnny and Robb's scam?"

"You mean Johnny contacting Robb and telling him what we needed and Robb relaying orders to the moving bots and ships and rerouting them here?" asked Jake.

"Yes that," said Nicole.

"Naw. Although there might be some guy in New Glenbrook wondering what the hell happened to his barbecue grill when he gets back to Earth," said Jake. "Hopefully the one with that sign."

"I think all the stuff came from Washington though," said Nicole. "Remember? All the volleyballs had the presidential seal."

"That's right," said Jake. "I hope this doesn't mean I'm going to get audited every year now. You know I think I've done my bit for king and planet. Maybe now my mom will finally stop saying I don't do enough pro-bono work."

Chapter Thirty-One

Robb threw yet another ringer at the formerly Larson and now Anderson farm horseshoe pit and he and Johnny celebrated as Varcus looked on.

"There you are. What's up, big guy?" Jake asked as he handed Varcus a cup of rum punch.

"Nothing is up," said Varcus somberly.

"You're not still sore about us humans being back on Earth, are you?" asked Jake. Varcus looked at him and Jake immediately felt a twinge of guilt. "I know, we kind of blackmailed you, but aren't you the least bit happy for us?"

"Of course I am. You're very nice beings. But this was bigger than you," said Varcus. "You know it's not always about just you humans you know."

"Yeah but we're here now. And it's a beautiful Earth night, Steve and Cynthia are throwing this great barn dance slash luau, there's a great band...what is there to worry about?" said Jake.

Varcus gave Jake that look again and Jake stopped smiling. "Yeah I know, there's still the whole environmental thing. Look, I'm gonna do everything I can to make sure we get things working right here on Earth."

Varcus continued to stare at Jake and Jake considered squirming. "I mean it," he said instead, meaning it. "I've got this whole celebrity Representative thing going for me now and I'm going to use it to fight eco evil doers."

"That makes me feel better, Jake," said Varcus. "I believe you'll do just that."

"Good," said Jake, feeling relieved for some reason. "You know you should teach me that look you do. I could go around the planet getting CEOs to lower their company's emissions in a heartbeat."

"What look?" asked Varcus.

"That look you were just giving me. That *you've been very, very naughty and you should feel very, very guilty about it* look," said Jake.

"Oh that look," said Varcus, taking a drink of his punch. "To learn it you'd need to break your Vandorian mother's three hundred year old Actadel marriage vase playing womball in the house and then try to blame it on your goofur."

"Never mind then, I don't own a goofur," said Jake. "Let's go inside where the party is instead." They did so and Varcus excused himself to go get a plate of roast pig and sweet corn.

Jake spied Larry looking gloomy over in the corner and went over to him.

"Now what's wrong with you?" said Jake.

Larry pointed at Tommy and Paula out on the dance floor. "What does he have that I don't have? Besides two less arms and a lot less manliness."

Jake watched them for a moment. "I don't know, but I'm pretty sure they're just friends no matter what Tommy might be hoping."

"Well in spite of my obvious superiority to him she won't have anything to do with me," said Larry sulkily. "I think she still wants me to sign a metaphysical exclusive rights agreement with her so perhaps I will just give up on trying to woo her again. It would put too great a strain on the relationship between me and my libido to say goodbye to all the other chicks out there."

"Your choice. She's a pretty nice looking catch though," said Jake.

"Yes she is. But I think I like the fishing part better," said Larry. He looked off into the distance and looked unhappy again.

"Now what?" said Jake. "Boy you aliens are a moody bunch tonight. Robb is the only one in a good mood and that's just plain weird."

"I was thinking about my pizza parlor," said Larry. "And how it won't be a pizza parlor now and will only be a planet instead."

"Oh that. Well can't you just do it without us?" said Jake.

"No. It's against interstellar copyright laws to make a profit from any original idea of an alien species," said Larry. "Having you humans live and work there would have made it legal, but now I would have to give the billions upon billions of pizzas away and that would make earning back my setup costs most difficult. But it's the pizza I will miss the most. Kneading the floury dough with my hands, pouring on the rich red sauce as I slowly rotate the pan, sprinkling on the majestic cheese, carefully placing the thinly sliced spicy pepperoni in an eye pleasing pattern..." said Larry, becoming all misty eyed.

"Would you like to be alone with your pie?" asked Jake.

"I will miss it all so much!" said Larry, starting to tear up.

"Look. I can't believe I'm about to say this," said Jake. "I have an uncle back in Chicago who runs a little pizzeria around the corner from my place downtown. Great Chicago style pie. He's been wanting to get out of the business for some time now and move to Tampa where it's warm but he's been having trouble finding a buyer with this economy. If you're interested I could get you two together and--"

"Me?! Buy a pizza place on Earth? That thought had never entered my overly large brain," said Larry. "I guess my thought patterns tend towards the really big ideas and miss out sometimes on the little smaller ideas that are actually more aesthetically pleasing and--"

"Yeah, yeah, yeah," interrupted Jake. "Would you be interested or not?"

"Yes," whimpered Larry happily, eyes full of tears. "Thank you!" he said and wrapped all four arms around Jake before he could stop him and gave him a long and not so manly hug. "I must go outside now and hide my wet optic marbles before my chromosome patterns come under questioning," he said and rushed out the door of the barn.

"I see you and Larry are bonding," said Nicole, coming up behind Jake. "How was the hug?"

"Disturbingly beguiling," said Jake. "I can unfortunately see now why women like those quadruple limbs of his."

"Should I be jealous?" asked Nicole.

"Maybe. I get the feeling I'm going to be seeing a lot of him in the future," said Jake worriedly.

"Dudes! You gotta see this," said Johnny walking up with Robb. "Go ahead and show 'em, Robodude."

Robb put the skateboard he was carrying down on the wooden barn floor and stepped gingerly onto it. He crouched slowly and carefully then jumped and tried to do an Ollie but got tangled up in the landing and crashed to the ground with a loud clatter. "Ouch," he said.

"He's supposed to do that right?" said Jake.

"What do you mean?" said Johnny.

"Fall down and hurt himself. I see you skater types do that all the time," said Jake.

"Yeah, it's part of the fun," said Johnny.

Robb got up and brushed himself off. "Yes, it's part of the fun I have not gotten used to quite yet."

"You'll have lots of time, dude," said Johnny. "Did you hear? Varcus said Robb can stay on Earth with me!"

"Really? How does your mom feel about that?" asked Nicole.

"She was pretty sore until Robb vacuumed the house, did the dishes and the laundry and took out the garbage," said Johnny. "Now I think she wants to adopt him."

"Your birth parent is very nice," said Robb. "You should appreciate her more."

"Oh Yeah? If you thought Varcus was bossy just wait," said Johnny. "Come on, let's go back outside. Those two old timers wanted to play another round of shoes, double or nothing."

"Alright. But I feel guilty about taking their money," said Robb.

"Do you want your own board or not?" asked Johnny, heading towards the door. "Hurry before they change their minds."

Varcus strolled up with a plate of food and a barbecue sauce goatee. "Has anyone seen Steve or Cynthia? I just have to have this delicious pig recipe."

"I think they're in the house," said Nicole.

"What, again?" asked Jake. "Are they trying to set some sort of record?"

"Well they're newlyweds now," said Nicole.

"Yeah but they've been living together in sin for almost a year," said Jake. "It can't be that different."

"Cynthia did say something about her biological clock getting jump started with all this Earth and life talk," said Nicole.

"Oh sure. Varcus just gets finished putting all us messy humans back on the planet and the first thing they want to do is manufacture more of us," said Jake.

"Yes," said Nicole.

"Speaking of manufactured beings I hear you ditched Robb, Varcus," said Jake.

"Umm, yes," said Varcus. "It's borderline illegal for me to leave him here but it's what he wanted."

"Well it was borderline illegal for you to leave us here too," said Jake. "Hey does this make us all illegal aliens now?"

"I suppose it does," said Varcus.

"Cool," said Jake.

Larry came back inside and stood next to Jake and struck his manliest pose.

"All better now?" asked Jake.

"Yes, thank you," said Larry.

"Would you like to dance?" asked Nicole.

"Sure!" said Larry happily.

"Not you, Larry," said Nicole, exasperated with him by now. "I meant Jake."

"How about a rain check?" said Jake. "I've been meaning to ask Larry here something."

"Alright. Varcus?" said Nicole.

"It would be my pleasure," said Varcus and he presented an arm for Nicole to take. She did so and they disappeared onto the crowded dance floor, except for Varcus' head and shoulders of course.

"So. What did you want to ask me, best buddy?" asked Larry.

"Best buddy?" said Jake.

"Yes," said Larry. "I was thinking since I am going to be working in the neighborhood where you live we can be BFFL's and do all sorts of manly things together, go to football games, drink beer, pick up chicks, go to the bingo hall..."

"We'll see about that. Anyway, I've been wondering," said Jake. "And since we're suddenly best friends you can level with me. Your planet, Aurora. Was it really as nice as it looked?"

"Yes. Definitely," said Larry.

"Really?" said Jake skeptically.

"Really," said Larry. "Well that one island anyway."

"That's what I thought," said Jake.

"On the one side," said Larry.

"Uh-huh," said Jake.

"Especially after I changed the color of the sky in the 5D video," said Larry. "And of the water. And added that second sun. And tweaked the temperature about thirty degrees."

"Yep," said Jake.

"And turned all the mega-skeeters buzzing around into pretty birds," said Larry.

"Ever thought about going into real estate?" asked Jake.

"Naw," said Larry. "Not enough oregano."

Chapter Thirty-Two

Jake, Nicole and Cynthia stood in the driveway next to Steve's fully decorated *Just Married* pick-up truck, a *Wisconsin Dells or bust!* sign in the back window. Cynthia gave Nicole a hug, then walked over to Jake and gave him a big long squeeze. "Thanks, Jake. For everything," she said.

"No problem, girl," said Jake and Cynthia went around and got in the truck.

Steve reached out the window and shook hands with Jake. "See ya, buddy. Nicole's got the key. Just lock up and put it in the milk can when you leave. You guys can stay as long as you want."

"Thanks. I can use a vacation after all that," said Jake. "You guys have a good time. But keep him out of the sun, Cynthia. He burns in like two and a half minutes."

Cynthia smiled and Steve waved and put the truck in gear and they drove away.

"Better go say bye to the big guy," said Jake. "You want to come?"

"Varcus and I already said our goodbyes," said Nicole. "Besides, you two should be alone anyway in case you want to get all mushy."

Jake walked across the yard and up to the top of the ramp of the ship where Varcus was standing waving goodbye to Steve and Cynthia.

"Great party last night, Jake," said Varcus. "Was Cynthia upset about her cows?"

"A little, but lucky for you she was too excited about the honeymoon to do anything about it," said Jake.

"Well, I'm sorry anyway. I guess I got carried away," said Varcus.

"Is their milk going to be colored too?" asked Jake. "You know, green from the green cows, pink from the pink cows, etc."

"I'm afraid so," said Varcus. "But it won't affect the taste. And it should wear off in a few days. Or maybe weeks. Hopefully not months."

"Hey, don't sweat it. That's what cows are for. Milking, eating and abusing," said Jake.

"Evidently," said Varcus. "I see Larry is gone. Did he go home?"

"Yeah he went to get all his things, especially his lucky oven mitt," said Jake.

"Good old Larry," said Varcus. "Having him in your neighborhood should prove most interesting."

"That's one way to put it," said Jake.

The two fell silent for a moment and Varcus and Jake looked at one another. "We've come far, you and me," said Varcus.

"Yes we have," said Jake. "Hey wait a minute, where have I heard that before?"

Varcus sighed. "Okay, it's from *Dances with Wolves*," he admitted. "You know, at the end? Where Kicking Bird is talking to Dances with Wolves..."

"Right, that's it. Great movie," said Jake.

"Great screenplay. Michael Blake. I just always wanted to say it," said Varcus. "But this is it I guess. It's been--"

"Educational," finished Jake.

"I hope so. Take care," said Varcus. He put out a giant hand towards Jake and Jake gladly took it and shook it, then Varcus suddenly gave Jake the manliest hug of his life.

"You too, Varcus," said Jake when he was finally set free. "If you're ever in the neighborhood give me a call. We'll catch a Cubs game. You, me and Larry."

"I'll do that. Goodbye, Jake," said Varcus and he stepped inside his ship and Jake turned and walked down the ramp, then stopped at the bottom and turned.

"Hey you gonna do the time travel thing again?" said Jake. "Jump ahead ten, twenty years and see what happens to us?"

Varcus stuck his head back outside the door. "No I think I'll stick around the area for a while. I want to see what your people can do."

"Me too," said Jake. He walked over to Nicole and they stood watching and waving as Varcus' ship glided silently up into the blue sky and disappeared.

Nicole looked around at the farm which suddenly looked surprisingly ordinary, except for the herd of rainbow colored bovines. "Alone at last."

"Yep. Not an alien in sight," said Jake.

"Nope. So what now?" asked Nicole.

"What now?" said Jake. "Now I think I'm going to take a look at environmental law. And you've got a few photos to show to someone."

"That sounds great," said Nicole. "But that's not what I meant."

"Well what did you mean?" asked Jake.

"I meant right now, now. What should we do now?" said Nicole.

Jake thought about it for a moment. "I don't know about you but I could really go for some pizza."

"Yeah I'm famished," said Nicole. "Do you want to drive?"

Jake put his arm around Nicole's waist and looked around at the beautiful Earth day. "Naw," he said. "Let's walk."

The End